"Please, don't worry about me,"

Amy said.

"I can't help myself," Mike replied with a sigh, feeling his self-control slipping. Resist, he ordered himself. Don't let her get to you.

But even as he cautioned himself, Mike realized it was too late. Amy had reached deep within and touched a tender part of him that he seldom acknowledged. It wasn't simply worry about her that was affecting him. It was more. Much more.

Slowly, Mike lowered his head and touched his lips to hers. The taste of vanilla lingered there, reminding him of the way she'd licked ice cream off her fingers just a little while before. They were alone, and she was too close, too appealing, too perfect.

Mike deepened the kiss....

Dear Reader:

Happy holidays! Our authors join me in wishing you all the best for a joyful, loving holiday season with your family and friends. And while celebrating the new year—and the new decade!—I hope you'll think of Silhouette Books.

1990 promises to be especially happy here. This year marks our tenth anniversary, and we're planning a celebration! To symbolize the timelessness of love, as well as the modern gift of the tenth anniversary, each month in 1990, we're presenting readers with a *Diamond Jubilee* Silhouette Romance title, penned by one of your all-time favorite Silhouette Romance authors.

In January, under the Silhouette Romance line's *Diamond Jubilee* emblem, look for Diana Palmer's next book in her bestselling LONG, TALL TEXANS series—*Ethan*. He's a hero sure to lasso your heart! And just in time for Valentine's Day, Brittany Young has written *The Ambassador's Daughter*. Spend the most romantic month of the year in France, the setting for this magical classic. Victoria Glenn, Annette Broadrick, Peggy Webb, Dixie Browning, Phyllis Halldorson—to name just a few!—have written *Diamond Jubilee* titles especially for you. And Pepper Adams has penned a trilogy about three very rugged heroes—and their lovely heroines!—set on the plains of Oklahoma. Look for the first book this summer.

The *Diamond Jubilee* celebration is Silhouette Romance's way of saying thanks to you, our readers. We've been together for ten years now, and with the support you've given us, you can look forward to many more years of heartwarming, poignant love stories.

I hope you'll enjoy this book and all of the stories to come. Come home to romance—Silhouette Romance—for always!

Sincerely,

Tara Hughes Gavin
Senior Editor

VAL WHISENAND

Giveaway
Girl

Published by Silhouette Books New York
America's Publisher of Contemporary Romance

To Gary, Rita and Michelle;
Karen, Rick and Joshua;
and to Joe, who started it all

SILHOUETTE BOOKS
300 E. 42nd St., New York, N.Y. 10017

ISBN: 0-373-08695-4

First Silhouette Books printing January 1990

Printed in the U.S.A.

VAL WHISENAND

is an incurable romantic, married to her high school sweetheart since she was seventeen. The mother of two grown children, she lives in a house she designed and which she and her husband built with their own two hands. Her varied interests have led her to explore many fascinating occupations and travel throughout the United States and Canada. Whether her goal is to write another book, learn a foreign language or prevail over tremendous odds to become a winning game show contestant, her natural tenacity sees to it that she succeeds. Once she makes up her mind, there's no stopping her!

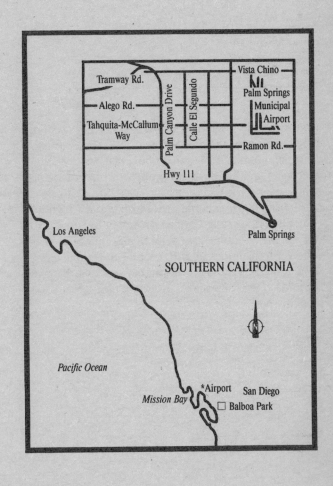

Tramway Rd.

Alego Rd.

Tahquita-McCallum Way

Palm Canyon Drive

Calle El Segundo

Vista Chino

Palm Springs

Municipal Airport

Ramon Rd.

Hwy 111

Palm Springs

Los Angeles

SOUTHERN CALIFORNIA

Pacific Ocean

Mission Bay

*Airport

San Diego

☐ Balboa Park

N

Chapter One

Amy Alexander sighed as she stood in the Palm Springs sunshine checking the address on the business card she clutched in her hand. She knew if she didn't gather her courage and follow through with her idea, she'd never find out if Mike Dixon could help her.

Amy pushed her reddish-blond hair out of her eyes and quickly entered the fifties-style office building, pausing at the door marked Search International while she struggled to calm her racing imagination. It wasn't too late to change her mind, she reasoned. Impulse had brought her there, and contradictory impulse could as easily carry her far away.

Before she had time to come to a decision, the office door was opened from the inside, and a tall, good-looking man in a heather-gray sport jacket and slacks nearly bumped into her. Startled, Amy jumped back.

His smile was broad and welcoming. "Oops. Excuse me, Ms....." He stared at Amy. "Say, haven't I seen you at Marino's?"

She nodded. "Yes."

Oh, yes, he mused. There was no mistaking the young woman's soft beauty and strikingly blue eyes *or* the antique gold and ruby wedding band on the third finger of her left hand. And she was dressed the way he was used to seeing her, too, in a silky white blouse and slim, dark skirt.

Amy smiled as she recognized the steady customer her female employees vied to serve. No wonder, she thought. He was even more personable up close than across the crowded dining room of the restaurant.

She extended her hand. "Actually, I'm the manager at Marino's. My name is Amy Alexander, but please, call me Amy." She glanced down at the business card still cradled in her palm. "I assume you're Mike Dixon?"

"Yes." Mike shook her hand firmly. "To what do I owe the pleasure of your visit? Did I forget to leave a tip yesterday?"

Amy was taken with Mike's unaffected friendliness. He was going to be easy to talk to, to confide in, and she began to congratulate herself on her decision to come to him for help.

"Actually," Amy said, "this is business."

He stepped back, gesturing for her to enter the small office. "I must apologize. My secretary didn't tell me I had another appointment before lunch."

"You didn't," Amy said. "I was afraid that if I had to wait to see you I might change my mind, so I didn't make an appointment." When she turned and looked up at him she saw curiosity and patient understanding in the deep brown of his eyes.

"As luck would have it, I'm free until two," Mike said. "Please, sit down, won't you?"

Amy laughed nervously. "To tell you the truth, I'd rather pace the floor. I've had an unbelievable week."

I can see you have, Mike thought. Missing were her animated personality, her usual friendly smile and her bouncy air. Oh, her shoulder-length hair still sparkled with golden highlights, but some of the fire had gone out of her eyes, and she was far too pale. Whatever had happened to her, it had shaken her to the core.

When he saw her tremble, he suggested, "Let's pace together, then. I was about to head over to the famous Marino's for lunch, and I think the walk will do us both good. How about it? You can tell me what's bothering you on the way."

Nodding, Amy agreed. "All right. Only how about grabbing a hamburger, instead? This morning I chose your business card from the entrants in our weekly complimentary businessman's lunch contest. I wouldn't want anyone to see us together and doubt the fairness of our drawing."

Mike's laugh was vibrant as he escorted her into the hall. "You're kidding! I won? I'll bet I've put three dozen cards in that fishbowl at Marino's. It's about time."

"The timing couldn't have been better for me, personally," Amy confessed. "If I hadn't drawn your card I might not have noticed your profession." She waited while he locked the office door behind them.

Leading the way into the street, Mike squinted in the brightness and slipped on his sunglasses. "Nice day. Spring in the California desert is my favorite season."

"Yes," Amy agreed. "I'm afraid I was so wrapped up in my thoughts on the way over here, I didn't notice. It is a pretty day."

Mike gestured to her. "Then come on. A brisk walk will raise your spirits. Besides, I feel like we're old friends since we have Marino's in common. It's a great restaurant."

Keeping pace with Mike's long strides, letting the warm sun bathe her in its rays, Amy felt a renewal of strength, a calming of her soul. For the first time since her accidental discovery of the truth she found herself believing there was a chance she could sort out her confusing past.

They'd walked nearly a block as silent companions before Amy was ready to initiate conversation. "Is it true you locate missing persons?" By the time she had completed the sentence a quiver had crept into her voice.

Mike glanced at her. "I try."

Surprised and disgusted by the strong effect her simple opening question was having on her emotions, Amy took a deep, shaky breath and blinked hard. "Damn. I'm sorry. I thought I was ready for this."

The sight of her misty eyes spurred him to offer moral support. "It's all right. Take your time." He eyed her wedding band. "Is your husband the one who's missing?"

"My what?"

Mike pointed to the ring. "Your husband."

"Oh, no," Amy told him. She managed to smile slightly at his quizzical expression. "I have no husband." Her smile grew. "I never did."

"But . . ." Mike recalled the first time he'd seen Amy and how the presence of the ring had put an immediate end to his plans to approach her.

Amy's voice lowered. "The ring was my mother's." Pensively she twisted the gold band while she gazed at it. "When Mom died, she wanted me to have it. Wearing it seemed the best way to remember her."

Walking beside Amy, Mike stuffed his hands into the pockets of his wool slacks. "And it kept you safer at work. Right?"

"Perhaps. I have a rule that I never date Marino's clientele. Mother's ring gives me a plausible reason to refuse without hurting anyone's feelings." Amy looked up at him, studying his stern expression. "I'm sure you understand."

Smiling and nodding, Mike agreed. "Of course. I have the same basic rule. Which reminds me, you still haven't told me who it is you want me to find." Once again moisture began to fill Amy's eyes.

"My real parents," she said with a nervous hush in her voice. "I've discovered I'm adopted."

* * *

Amy stood at Mike's elbow. "I still wish you'd reconsider and let me pay for half," she said, watching him peel off a few bills and pass them to the counter girl at the hamburger stand.

"Nonsense. I could feed half a dozen people here for the price of a good dinner at Marino's."

"We're not *that* expensive," Amy protested.

Mike chuckled. "You're right. Marino's is one of the most moderately priced of the fine restaurants in Palm Springs. That's why I frequent it." He gestured over his shoulder. "Why don't you go grab us a table, and I'll bring the food?"

"Okay."

She chose a place by a window and watched Mike's broad back as he lifted their tray and started toward her, weaving his way smoothly through the array of crowded, colorful plastic tables. Burgers in paper boxes were stacked four deep on the orange tray, and two large orders of fries had spilled on the paper tray cover.

She protested when he unloaded half the food in front of her. "I told you I wasn't hungry."

Mike smiled. "You have to eat."

Setting a large paper cup in front of her, he slipped into the swivel chair opposite hers. "There's a chocolate malt, too, to keep up your strength."

"Who says I haven't been?"

Mike opened a burger box and placed it next to the malt. "I do. I'm a sleuth, remember? I know these things."

"Nonsense. I'm fine. I'm just a little upset right now."

"And well you should be, considering what you told me on the way over here," Mike said. "Now, come on. Dig in so I can. I'm starving."

Obligingly, Amy lifted the hamburger and forced herself to take a bite. As much as she hated to admit it, Mike was right. She hadn't been eating properly, nor had she been sleeping—not since she'd opened that cursed box and found her mother's records of her childhood.

Amy bit into the hamburger again then put it down.

"There. That's better." Mike wiped his mouth with a napkin. "So, what happened after your father died and his lawyer deliverd the box of personal papers to you?"

"Nothing at first. I wasn't ready to go through them and I really had no need to. When he had his first stroke, Daddy gave me all the information I'd need to administer his small estate."

"So you left the box unopened?"

"Until a week ago last Sunday."

"And then?"

Amy took a sip of her malt wishing it was a soft drink to help wash down the lump in her throat. She leaned forward, her hands clasped in front of her on the table, and looked into Mike's eyes.

"I'd forgotten all about the box. I was cleaning up some of my father's belongings, preparing to take them to the patients at Oak Knoll Convalescent Hospital, when I came across it again." She sighed. "That's when I made my big mistake."

"You opened it."

"Yes." Turning away, Amy stared at the passing traffic on Palm Canyon Drive. "Oh, God, I wish I hadn't."

"Your actions were perfectly logical," Mike said. "You had no way of knowing what you'd find."

"I know." She turned to him. "There was a pink-covered scrapbook along with some packets of old letters and newspaper clippings. I ignored the other stuff, but the book had my name on the cover. Naturally, I opened it."

"And that's where you learned you'd been adopted?"

"Yes." Shaking her head Amy exhaled sharply. "At first I didn't believe it. I just kept reading my mother's account of it over and over." She dabbed at a tear that had slipped down her cheek. "I'm sorry. I thought I was ready to explore all this."

"Do you need me to tell you you're not?"

"I—I guess not. But what should I do?"

"Professional opinion?"

"Of course." Amy was touched by the genuine concern she saw on Mike's face.

"Let it go. Forget it." He knew his suggestion was sensible. He also knew, from the look in Amy's eyes, that she wasn't going to take his advice, sound or not.

"I can't."

"I'd assumed as much." Mike leaned back in his chair. "Then how about this? Suppose you promise yourself a six-month cooling-off period? At the end of that time, if you still want to pursue your roots, we'll pull out all the stops."

Amy reached absently for a French fry and bit off the end. "I don't know. Six months is an awfully long time."

"Not when you compare it to a lifetime."

"I guess not."

"Besides," Mike said, smiling, "I told you I never date clients."

Amy cocked her head. "I beg your pardon?"

"Date. You and me. You know. Socially?" He smiled across the small table. "I'd like the opportunity to treat you to a little more elegant meal."

Reaching for another fry, Amy averted her gaze. There was too much already going on in her life, in her mind. Too much turbulence. Too many confusing feelings. This was not the time for a new relationship, however casual, and looking at Mike Dixon, she doubted anything about him was quite as simple as it might seem on the surface. She blushed, remembering the funny little jolt of adrenaline she used to get when he dined at Marino's and she sensed he was watching her work.

If he were less appealing she might chance accepting his invitation as a pleasant diversion. As it was, her overloaded consciousness couldn't stand any more strain, and she knew it.

Amy smiled at him. "I'm sorry. I told you *I* never date the customers."

Mike raised his hands, his open palms toward her. "I swear I'll never eat in Marino's again. Scout's honor."

"You can't do that!"

"Why not? Think of the money I'll save."

Amy had to chuckle. "That's quite a sacrifice to offer to make, but it won't be necessary."

"You're going to change your policy?"

"No, I'm not. I simply meant I don't want you giving up your favorite restaurant on account of me. Especially not Marino's."

He cocked his head, raising one eyebrow. "I'm not your type?"

Something in his demeanor gave Amy pause. The smile was still in place on his face, yet there had been a subtle change in him. Amy began to think she might have hurt his feelings by refusing his invitation to dinner.

She softened. If any man was her "type," Mike Dixon definitely was. And she reasoned it would be unkind not to tell him so. "On the contrary," she began, a deeper blush stealing up her cheeks, "I find you very...interesting."

He settled back. "Thank you."

The remnants of a smile quirked the corners of his mouth, and Amy noticed for the first time a faint scar on his cheek. Rather than detract from his appearance, it gave him a roguish air she hadn't been conscious of before. When his fingers lightly brushed the small mark she realized she'd been staring.

"I—I'm sorry. I didn't mean to be impolite."

Mike rose with a nonchalant shrug. "Don't worry about it." He glanced at his watch. "Sorry, but I'm afraid I do have to be going. I have a two o'clock appointment at the airport."

"No problem. I'm finished," Amy said, gathering her leftover lunch into a neat pile on the tray.

"You could take this home to your dog."

"Except I don't have one." Amy followed Mike to the receptacle as he disposed of their trash. "Besides, you can imagine how my staff would tease me if I showed up at Marino's carrying a paper sack from *this* place."

"You'd probably be run out of town on a rail," Mike offered. "I certainly wouldn't want to be responsible for that." He held the door for her then followed her outside. "Have you given my earlier suggestion about your problem some thought?"

"You mean waiting six months to look for my parents?" She shaded her eyes with her hand. "Yes. I suppose you're right."

"You know I am."

They began the walk back while Amy searched her heart for a better understanding of what inner force was compelling her. "Do you deal with a lot of people in my situation?" she finally asked.

"Enough. Although most of them have known about their origins for some time."

"But . . ." Amy hesitated. "You're going to think I'm crazy, but I have to ask. Do the others, the adopted ones, feel sort of lost, almost as if they didn't exist or weren't real?" Gaining courage, she went on. "It's weird. I mean, one minute I'm the daughter of Martha and Ray Alexander with a family history and a concrete past and the next minute it's as if I don't know who I am. As if I never *did* know."

He stopped her with a quick, light touch on her arm. "It's not crazy."

"I—I feel like I'm coming apart, Mike." She looked up at him. "And I don't know what to do about it."

"That's why I want you to wait a while," he said. "Give it time. Sleep on it." He smiled slightly at her wide-eyed expression. "You'll notice I didn't tell you to forget about your adoption by the Alexanders. That would be impossible. All I ask is that you let the newness wear off; let time soothe the trauma until you're thinking rationally.''

"Do you think I'll get over it? Is that what you're saying?'' Mike had started to walk again, and Amy had to scurry to keep up with his long, purposeful strides.

"No, Ms. Alexander, I don't,'' he said. "I'm sorry but I think your unfortunate situation is quite permanent.''

"That's what I was afraid of.''

"I wish I could offer a brighter outlook,'' he said gently. "Sometimes I tend to be a bit too pragmatic, I guess.''

"That's okay. I asked for the truth. I'm pretty used to dealing with reality.''

Amy thought about her father and how she truly missed his cantankerous grumbling and constant demands. She'd been so wrapped up in taking care of the ailing man she hadn't had the time or inclination to develop new relationships when she'd brought him to the desert for his health. He, and her work, had become her whole life, demanding her every waking thought.

True, she'd been imprisoned by her sense of duty but that imprisonment was softened by love and caring, by mutual trust and support. Now, rather than giving her cause to celebrate, her newfound freedom from responsibility had left her feeling alone and unfocused.

Amy looked up at the pure, blue sky. If losing loved ones through no fault of your own hurt so deeply, what a living hell it must be to have to voluntarily surrender your baby into the care of strangers!

The supper crowd at Marino's was typical of a Wednesday night; sufficient but undemanding. Low light from the crystal chandeliers reflected off the warmly papered walls and maroon carpet, while the last rays of daylight shone through stained-glass windows. The whole restaurant had a subtle ambience, an aura of richness.

Thankful for a respite from the usual rush of diners, Amy busied herself checking the change in the cash drawer to be sure her hostesses and cashier would have no problems later in the evening.

"I told you, it's not a big deal," Marissa said. "Go, already. I can close out without you."

"I know you can." Amy smiled at the bubbly, petite young woman she was grooming to become her assistant. "But I feel guilty when I don't personally supervise the daily operations."

Marissa shook her short, dark curls and made a face. "Phooey. How many times have you told me that a good manager delegates tasks so things will run smoothly no matter what?"

"Lots?" Amy was smiling.

"Millions."

"That many?" Amy finished her count, tucked the surplus cash into a zippered pouch and closed the cash drawer. "Then I may be right."

"You must be." Marissa took the pouch as she pushed Amy out from behind the counter. "The last run of the tram is at eight o'clock. If you don't hurry you won't make it."

Amy was almost convinced. "You're sure you don't mind?"

"I'm sure, already. I'm sure. I'll take good care of your precious customers for you."

The resonant male voice behind them made the hair on Amy's neck prickle.

"This customer insists on personal service, Ms. Alexander."

She whirled, her pulse beginning to speed. "Mike!" She was glad to see him. She'd been sorry all afternoon that she'd refused his overtures and not at all sure how to reverse the situation gracefully. "I thought you'd sworn off Marino's."

"Not if my absence won't get me a date, I haven't." Mike crossed the dimly lit entrance hall in three quick strides. "Therefore, I've decided to blitz you with my presence. I'm eating *every* meal here until you agree to go out with me."

Amy laughed softly. "We don't serve breakfast, Mr. Dixon."

"No problem. I'll bring donuts in a paper sack and sit on your fancy flagstone porch to eat them."

Smiling, Amy retrieved her purse from a cabinet beneath the counter. "I believe you would, too, so I guess it's up to me to save you from embarrassment and preserve Marino's reputation."

"You'll have dinner with me?" Mike's tone was incredulous. "I can't believe how easy that was. You're a pushover!"

"Wrong," Amy said. "I'm on my way to ride the Palm Springs Aerial Tramway to the top of Mount San Jacinto, and I'm willing to let you tag along if you want."

"The tram? That little metal bucket that hangs from a steel cable hundreds of feet above the gorge?" He scratched his head thoughtfully. "Wouldn't you rather do something safer, like run the Colorado River rapids or skydive without a parachute?"

"Nope. I like the tram. It's relaxing." She chuckled under her breath at the look on Mike's face. "And it's where I'm going tonight. If you're coming, we'll have to get a move on. The last complete run starts at eight. If we don't hurry we could miss it."

Mike nodded and offered her his arm. "Perish the thought, Ms. Alexander. We wouldn't want to miss the chance to dangle in space in a flimsy little box with dozens of other equally demented people, would we?"

"Speak for yourself, Mike Dixon," Amy quipped.

He held the door for her and rolled his eyes heavenward. "I was," Mike said evenly. "Believe me, I was."

Chapter Two

Amy's Jaguar took the curves of the mountainous approach to the tram station effortlessly. The powder-blue car wasn't new—far from it—yet it handled superbly.

She smiled at Mike's grip on the sides of the leather seat. "Does my driving bother you?"

"Oh, no," he said with exaggerated inflection.

"Good." Amy's hands caressed the steering wheel. "This car is the only real extravagance in my life. It cost me almost my entire inheritance but it was worth it. I practically stole it from one of our older restaurant clients by promising to treat it like a brother."

Mike raised one eyebrow at her. "In that case, I'm glad *I'm* not your brother."

Laughing, Amy downshifted for the steep climb past sage and occatillo plants and the stratified red and brown rocks barely discernible in her headlights. "So am I, Mike," she confessed, "but probably not for the same reason *you* meant." A sideways glance told her his left eyebrow had arched even higher, and the corner of his mouth was twitching mirthfully.

They were approaching the first of three parking areas at the tramway. "There are never any empty spots in A or B so I always park down here in lot C. But waiting for the shuttle takes far too long. Want me to let you off at the top of the hill or are you game to walk it with me?" Amy asked. "It's a pretty steep climb."

He snorted a chuckle. "How old do you think I am?"

"Oh, I don't know. Thirty-five?"

Scowling, he cast her a sidelong glance. "I'll be thirty in August."

"Oops. Sorry." Perhaps it wasn't so much his looks that had made him seem older than his actual years, but rather the fact he appeared so worldly-wise. Yet, she observed appreciatively, Mike was also a mature man in the sense that his body had developed to its fullest potential. His shoulders were broad, his waist narrow, his jaw square and his bearing that of someone totally self-assured and in command. In short, Amy mused, he was absolutely gorgeous!

"And you?" he asked.

"Huh?" She tried in vain to remember what it was they had been talking about.

"Your age. How old are you? Or is that already one of those secrets women insist on keeping?"

"Not at all. I'm twenty-three."

"A restaurant manager at your age?" Mike marveled. "Congratulations."

She whipped effortlessly into a parking place and shut off the motor. "I was precocious."

"Apparently. And brave, judging from your driving and your choice of recreation. Do you ride the tram often?"

"A lot, lately," Amy said, climbing out and locking her door. Mike followed suit. "I seem to do my best thinking in the solitude of the gondola, looking down at Palm Springs.

I guess the height tends to put everything into a better perspective."

She opened the car's trunk and exchanged her high heels for a pair of worn running shoes. She laced them quickly, then pulled on a pink sweater. Tugging it down around her hips, she eyed Mike. "I hope those shoes are comfortable."

"They'll do," he said. "Unless you happen to have a pair of size eleven men's Nikes in there, too."

"Sorry. I didn't know you were coming or I'd have planned ahead."

"Neither did I." Mike smiled a little sheepishly and considered his clothing. "Jeans would probably be better suited to a place like this."

"You're fine as you are," Amy observed honestly. She slung the strap of her purse over one shoulder. "Come on. I'll race you."

Mike started off at a trot, assuming he'd have to slow his pace to wait for Amy. Long before they reached the upper-level parking lot he realized how wrong he was. Leaning against the metal railing on the side of the stairs to the station he fought to catch his breath and calm the stitch in his side.

"Whew! You really know how to hurt a guy."

Also breathless, Amy bent forward, her hands resting on her knees. "I must confess . . . I may . . . have overdone it."

"No kidding!" When he glanced at her he found he couldn't bring himself to look away. Amy's eyes were sparkling, her cheeks the rosy pink he remembered. Her hair, always so perfectly combed and styled, was tousled in a thoroughly disarming manner. She seemed like a new person, no less appealing than before, just less inhibited, less careful to create the perfect image. He had to subdue the urge to grab her by the shoulders and kiss her soundly.

Amy straightened and smiled. "Come on. I don't want to miss my tram."

"That's okay." Glancing at the bubbling stream that flowed through a channel below the station, Mike refused to budge. "Just leave me here. There should be an ambulance along any minute to give me oxygen."

"Gripe, gripe, gripe." Laughing, Amy urged him up the stairs and through the heavy glass doors. "You wanted a date with me and you got one. So what's your problem?"

Mike was quickly regaining his energy but enjoyed teasing her. "I had hoped to be conscious during our time together," he said. "It's so much more fun that way."

She looped her arm through his. "You seem to be recovering nicely. You're not even gasping anymore."

"I never gasp," Mike countered. "At least not from running up a hill."

Amy decided it was time to change the subject. Through enormous windows they could see the entire tramway. Along it, lighted gondolas inched slowly up the mountain.

"There." She pointed. "Doesn't that look like fun?"

Logic told Mike the tram was as safe as a Sunday drive in the country. Probably *safer*, if the Sunday driver was Amy Alexander. His gut disagreed, but after seeing the childlike excitement in Amy's eyes he decided to rely on his more sensible thoughts.

"If it's what you want to do, then I'm willing," he said. "Where do I buy our tickets?"

"Over there." Amy pointed to a row of small windows along the east wall. One was open, and a line of passengers had formed in front of it.

"Good. Wait here. I'll be right back."

With her heart still skipping beats she watched him walk away. Being near Mike was exhilarating in the same way a trip to the circus or her birthday had been when she was a child. Anticipation alone was enough to make her short of breath, and she marveled at how good his presence made her feel when he was close by. Smiling, Amy wrapped her arms around herself and stared out the window at the hypnotic motion of the ascending silver and blue tram.

When Mike rejoined her she was so deep in thought she jumped at the sound of his voice.

"I didn't mean to startle you." He displayed their tickets. "I'm supposed to be the nervous one, remember?"

"Sorry." She shook her head. "I was just thinking and I guess I was pretty far away."

Together, they joined a line leading to the embarkation platform.

"Want to talk about it?" Mike asked.

Amy felt a warm glow flow through her body. True, her original thoughts had focused on Mike, but by the time he'd returned she'd also been thinking about her family. Now that Mike was beside her, the encroaching loneliness had fled enough that she was able to express her sentiments.

Pensive, Amy sighed as she watched the red, white and blue painted gondolas. "I came here the night I discovered my baby book. And I don't even remember getting on or off the tram."

Mike took her hand, pleased when she didn't resist.

"I just sat up there," she went on, squeezing his fingers and enjoying the strength of his grasp, "looking at all the bright lights of Palm Springs and wondering how many women down here had given up babies. I wondered whether they cared what eventually became of them—whether my real mother cares about me."

"The ones who gave you up are called 'birth parents,' Amy," Mike told her. "The Alexanders were your *real* parents."

A loving smile lifted the corners of her mouth. "I know that. They're both gone, now, but they'll always be first in my heart."

He guided her ahead of him as they boarded the gondola and rested his arm along the back of her seat as soon as they were settled. A full load of fellow travelers crowded in with them, and Amy scooted closer to Mike to make room for a family of four on the bench beside her.

"You're lucky to have experienced parental love," Mike said as he too, watched the interaction of the complete family next to her. "Many children never have what the Alexanders gave to you."

"I know." She leaned closer. "I just don't understand why they felt they couldn't tell me I was adopted. Surely, they must have known I'd find out eventually."

The tram swung free of the platform, lurching ahead while Mike braced himself. "Maybe not. You said the illness that took your mother was sudden, and shortly thereafter your father had an incapacitating stroke. Maybe they intended to destroy all the evidence and just never got around to it."

"Maybe. I suppose they did have to preserve some of the legal papers while I was still a minor." She smiled at Mike. "But enough about all that. Tell me about yourself."

"There's not much to tell. I lead a pretty normal life." Mike noticed the valley receding outside the gondola and added, "Most of the time."

"Then what about *your* childhood. I'll bet you were a cute little boy."

Mike felt his gut tying in knots and fought to hide his feelings. Childhood? That was a laugh. Nightmare was more like it.

"Well?" Amy prodded.

"I was darling," Mike finally said. "All the girls in the third grade fell for me."

I can believe *that*, Amy mused. Oh, yes. Smiling, she stared at the tram station as it grew smaller and smaller in the distance.

"I guess I had my first real crush in the eighth grade," she recalled. "He was an older man. An unrequited love." She giggled. "He was the school janitor. I used to bring him cookies I'd baked myself. You can imagine how disappointed I was when my family moved before my freshman year of high school.''

"I can imagine." A lopsided smile lifted the corners of his mouth.

"You're laughing at me."

"Not at all," Mike insisted. "I was just wondering how long it will be before you bake cookies for me."

"Why, Mr. Dixon. I hardly know you," she said with mock dismay. "Certainly you don't expect cookies after one date."

"At this point, I'd probably eat plate and all." Mike groaned. "I'm starving."

"There's a nice restaurant at the top of the mountain," Amy said. "I'm sure they stay open to accommodate the last runs of the tram."

"As it happens, Ms. Alexander, I was clever enough to notice the sign on the ticket booth and purchase the ride-and-dine package. Would you care to join me for dinner?"

A broad, happy smile spread across Amy's face. "I'd *love* to. I believe I'm actually hungry for a change."

Dinner was served promptly and efficiently. An enormous stone fireplace dominated one end of the spacious dining room, and Amy occasionally looked into the relaxing flames while she talked.

What the restaurant lacked in refinement it more than made up for with the fire and a spectacular view of the desert floor. Palm Springs twinkled below in a diagonal grid of brightly lit streets surrounded by the velvet blackness of the mountain ranges and night sky.

Outside, on the mountainside, a path led the more adventurous to descend to a warming hut intended for the intrepid hikers who journeyed to the peak the hard way, on the trail from the valley floor.

Finishing her coffee, Amy blotted her lips and laid the napkin beside her plate.

"So," Mike said, "you moved around a lot?"

"Uh-huh. I don't even remember all the towns we eventually lived in."

"And that didn't seem strange to you?"

She shrugged. "Not really. Dad did some kind of legal research for a law firm in Nevada. I never did understand what, exactly. I guess we moved so he could be close to wherever he was working at the time."

"And he didn't discuss the details of his work? Not even with your mother?" Mike noticed he was scowling and forced himself to relax his expression.

"No." Amy pushed her chair back and stood as the call for the last returning tram came over a loudspeaker. "Mother always said he deserved peace and quiet when he got home and I shouldn't bother him with questions." She shrugged. "After a while it became an unwritten law, 'Don't talk business to Dad.'"

"Curious," Mike mumbled, laying crisp bills on the polished wooden table. "Very curious."

Amy had preceded him to the door. "What did you say?"

"Nothing." Mike shook his head. "It's not important. Listen, I'll be out of town until a week from Tuesday, but when I get back I thought maybe you'd like me to go through the rest of your father's papers for you."

"I thought you said I should wait?"

He opened the door for her and followed her through. "I did. I still think you should. But there's no harm in doing some groundwork to see where we stand."

The cold, night air made Amy shiver in spite of her sweater, and Mike opened his coat to enclose her next to his chest as he stood behind her in the boarding line. He wrapped his arms around her, his lips brushing against fine strands of her hair that were lifted by the wind.

"I don't want to hire you," Amy said, leaning back and folding her arms beneath Mike's.

Placing a barely felt kiss on the top of her head he said, "Tell me you're saying that because I don't date clients and you'd like to spend more time with me."

"Am I so easy to read?" Amy twisted within his grasp to look into his eyes.

"Pretty easy."

"Well, I want you to know that I wouldn't be cuddling up to you like this if I weren't freezing," she insisted, turning away so Mike couldn't see her smiling. Thank goodness for low temperatures!

"I'll remember that, and always take you to places where our breath makes clouds in the air," he said, holding her to him. "Since this mountain is thousands of feet above the valley and consistently cold, I guess we'll have to come here a lot, won't we?"

Amy laughed softly. She leaned her head against his broad chest and gazed at him. His chin was starting to show a bit of stubble, his eyes were twinkling mischievously and his appealing mouth was so close it took her breath away.

"I don't think it will always be necessary for us to rely on cold weather," she said quietly.

"Neither do I," Mike whispered.

He lowered his head and covered her soft lips with his own in the briefest, sweetest kiss Amy had ever experienced. She quivered as the effects of Mike's tenderness danced along her sensitive nerves, joined forces to make her heart flutter erratically, then came to rest in her core as a tingly, quite unsettling surprise.

Her sigh was barely audible but Mike felt her shiver. "You're still cold." He started to release her. "Here, take my jacket."

Grasping his wrists, Amy drew his arms around her. "No. Please. This is fine, really." She hesitated, adding softly, "I like it this way."

Mike held her tightly, resting his cheek against the silkiness of her hair. Yes. It *was* fine to be together. Everything about being with Amy was good. Perhaps too good. His subconscious warned him against beginning to care for her—for anyone—just as it always did. But Mike argued to himself that he needn't worry. He could keep his emotional distance and still enjoy the benefits of romancing a pretty woman.

Clenching his jaw, Mike stared absently at the lights in the valley. It didn't take a rocket scientist to see that Amy had already begun to trust him, to rely on him, to feel some measure of affection for him. And he was having a devil of a time viewing her as just another convenient partner. He sensed what she was feeling. He hurt for her when she spoke of her life's trauma. He cared.

And that wouldn't do.

Not at all.

Chapter Three

Days passed before the tingle of Mike's brief kiss left Amy's lips. Even after that, all Amy had to do to relive the thrill was picture his face, imagine the deep timbre of his voice, and everything happened again in excruciatingly lovely slow motion. It had been a moment to savor.

She sat alone in her austere office at Marino's, leaned her elbows on the mahogany desk and wondered why Mike hadn't tried to kiss her again. Short of throwing her arms around his neck and flinging herself at him, she'd given him every possible encouragement. Yet he had behaved as if their marvelous kiss had never happened. She blushed at the recurrence of the still-vivid memory, willing it out of her mind with little real conviction. Naturally it refused to be banished.

Shaking her head, Amy tried to concentrate on the pile of paperwork on her desk. Marino's head chef, Alonzo, had rejected two cases of fresh gulf shrimp, then thrown a tantrum over the fact that their supplier had taken too long to replace the order. It had required several phone calls on

Amy's part and a formal letter of apology before the angry supplier would agree to ship anything to them again.

She signed her name to a pile of purchase orders, closed the file and stared past the gold-framed photographs of her parents. According to her desk calendar, Mike had been gone for nearly two weeks. So why did it seem like literally years? Admittedly, it had been his idea to look over the box of papers her father had left. Yet he'd seemed so reluctant at the end of their evening together Amy wondered if she would hear from him at all.

"Reluctant?" Amy snorted. "That's probably the understatement of the week." When Mike had promised to telephone, his terse, "I'll call you when I can," had sounded more like the farewell of someone she would never see again. The hardest part for Amy was not knowing what she had done to make him decide to avoid her.

She had pushed back the burgundy leather chair and was standing behind her desk, holding Mike's business card and trying to make up her mind whether or not to telephone his office when there was a faint rap on her door.

"Come in."

Marissa opened the door wide enough to stick her head through. "Sorry. There's a problem, boss. A man out here is demanding he see you. Says he was promised a free lunch and didn't receive it." Marissa winked.

Amy's heart lodged in her throat. She slipped the card into her pocket and swallowed to relieve the sudden dryness in her throat. "Send him in."

A bit sheepishly, Mike sidled in and greeted her. "Hello. I'm sorry I took so long getting back to you. My business..."

Why, oh, why did he have to look so appealing? And why couldn't she control the fluttering of her pulse whenever he was around? Amy held up her hand, hoping it, too, wasn't shaking. "No apology is necessary. You don't work for me, remember?"

"But it is necessary." He stood straighter. "I've been back in Palm Springs for three days. I should have called."

So, she'd been right in assuming he'd decided to avoid her. Her heart sank. Amy could see Mike was struggling, and she attempted to ease the situation for both their sakes. She knew her smile was forced and unnatural but it was the best she could do.

"And now you're here to claim the free lunch we owe you." Her cardboard smile widened. "I'm afraid it's my fault you never received your gift certificate. I had your business card in my possession and forgot all about processing it as a winner."

"I didn't really come here for that."

"But you are here, and we do owe you the prize." Seating herself, she opened a side drawer, withdrew a scrolled certificate and quickly penned "Mike Dixon of Search International" in the blank spaces.

She held it out to him. "Here you are."

Mike circled her desk, took her hand and laid aside the paper. "I owe you an apology, Amy."

"No, you don't."

"Yes, I do." Pulling her to her feet he captured her other hand, too. His thumbs gently caressed her knuckles. "You were open and honest with me, and I treated you terribly."

Terribly? Amy's eyes widened. Mike had provided the most enjoyable, most memorable evening of her entire life. The only thing terrible was the disappointing thought that there would never be another like it.

Mike's lips quirked into a half-smile she'd come to associate with him. "You see, I promised I'd call you but I intended to do just the opposite."

"I know." Her knees were about to buckle, and her head was swimming from the pleasure of his closeness, but she forced herself to pull her hands away. "I've been given the brush-off before." She stepped back. "I fully understand."

"No. No, you don't," Mike said. He started to reach for her but when she stepped farther away he paused. Amy was wiser than he was. The less physical contact they had the better off they'd both be—*especially* him.

Mike nodded. "Okay. But Amy, the problem is not with you. It's with me."

"I don't see any problem. You've changed your mind about helping me, and that's fine. After all, we hardly know each other. Certainly, you're under no obligation."

Mike thrust his hands into his pockets. "But I *want* to be," he insisted. "I'd like to at least volunteer to help you with your problem." He raised one eyebrow. "Please?"

The lost-little-boy look in Mike's eyes touched Amy deeply. Whatever his reasons for his actions might have been it was obvious he truly wanted to make it up to her. She could no more deny him that chance than she could deny her desires to be near him.

"All right. When?"

"Now? Tonight? Tomorrow?" He'd take her wherever she wanted to go. As long as they stayed among crowds he wouldn't be tempted to kiss her again. He could then make satisfactory recompense for the insensitive way he'd taken leave from her after their tram ride.

Mike congratulated himself. His plan was perfect. Amy would be compensated adequately when he gave her free advice about her adoption, and he could walk away forever with a clear conscience.

Her broad smile was so endearing, he had to plunge his hands deeper into his pockets to keep himself from reaching for her hand again.

"How about tonight at my place?" she said brightly. "I don't get off till nine but we could have dessert together and I could show you Dad's papers as you suggested." She saw him stiffen. "Or we could skip that part. I mean, it's not necessary."

What could he say? He'd stupidly left the choice of locations for their meeting up to her, never dreaming she'd invite him to her home. If he refused to go there, Amy's feelings would be hurt. They'd be right back where they'd been before he'd had his brilliant idea.

"No. Your place is fine." He started for the door. "Shall I pick you up here?"

"You could follow me home if you like. Or I can give you my home address and you can meet me."

"I'll follow you," Mike said, his hand on the doorknob. "That way I'll be sure you're safely home."

"Okay." As Amy watched him turn away and close the door she smiled into the empty room. Everything about Mike Dixon was appealing, from his thick, brown hair and empathetic eyes to his strong arms, to his voice, which made her tingle all the way to her toes. It was unlike her to feel so much enthusiasm for a simple date, and she reveled in the excitement, in the anticipation of what the future might bring now that Mike Dixon had tumbled into her life.

She covered a nervous giggle with her fingertips. Mike might have decided to try to hide or deny the fact that he, too, was attracted to her but he couldn't fool her. Not one bit.

Apple pie, Amy decided. And vanilla ice cream. Both were available in Marino's kitchen and were easily transported. She'd commandeer one of Alonzo's famous pies before it was cut. He owed her a favor after the shrimp fiasco.

Boxed and tied with a string, the pie sat waiting for her on the stainless-steel counter next to the chest freezer in the restaurant's kitchen. Two assistants dressed in white were chopping fresh vegetables, while the infamous Alonzo alternately gave orders and talked to the hollandaise sauce he was stirring. Amy greeted everyone, dodged a hurrying waitress and picked up the ice-cream scoop beside the freezer.

She was leaning over and packing ice cream into a cardboard container when Alonzo began to shout curses in Italian. Waving a dripping spoon he passed Amy in a blur of white-coated fury.

"No! Stop!" she ordered, looking up just in time to prevent the rotund chef from beaning Mike with the spoon. "It's okay. He's a friend of mine."

Mike had to sidestep to inch his way past the human barricade. "Sorry. Your assistant told me it would be all right to track you down in here."

Amy straightened, amused. "It is."

"Is he as dangerous as he looks?" Mike asked, eyeing the fuming man who was slowly returning to the stove where an assistant had taken over his earlier task.

"Only when we let him handle sharp knives," she said. "Which is actually most of the time. You were lucky all he had in his hand was a spoon."

"That's what I was afraid of." Mike joined Amy beside the freezer. "Can I help?"

She handed him the container. "Nope. All done. Would you close this, please?" She laid aside the heavy metal scoop she'd been using. A tiny bit of ice cream clung to her fingertips. She licked them while she looked around for a towel.

Mike folded the top of the container and fastened it closed. Seeing Amy bending over the freezer had sent his imagination into overdrive. His breathing was already increasing when she began licking her fingers. Now, his reaction was growing even stronger. All afternoon he'd been telling himself there'd be no problem avoiding involvement when he went to Amy's home and was alone with her. What a fool he was.

Amy's lips were moist and inviting, her eyes sparkling, her skin so smooth and soft he could feel it beneath his fingers as clearly as if he were stroking her. Mike drew a deep breath. It was going to be a long, long evening.

She washed and dried her hands. "There. Ready?"

Mike tried to sound nonchalant. "Sure, but wouldn't you rather go dancing or something?"

Amy laughed lightly. "I can tell you haven't been on your feet all day, Mr. Dixon."

"A movie! How about a movie?"

Taking the pie, Amy ushered Mike out of the kitchen and to her office. Closing the door behind them she took the ice-cream container, placed it on top of the pie box, then put both on her desk, turned and faced him.

"All right. Confess. What's going on here?"

"I don't know what you mean," Mike said with a shrug.

"Yes, you do. And if you don't want to go to my place, then admit it."

"I never said that." Mike could feel himself being drawn to her like steel to a magnet. Except he wasn't made of steel, he reminded himself. He was all too human.

Amy took a step closer. "You didn't have to say it. I know you don't want to be here." Her voice was even, low.

"That's not true." Mike's hands came to rest on her shoulders. The shoulders he had sworn not to touch. She was soft, yet strong, and her hair smelled like roses. Dark lashes fringed her eyes, and in their blue depths he saw a plea for honesty he couldn't deny.

"Then what is it?" Amy whispered, transfixed by his nearness.

"It's me," Mike said. "I was afraid I'd do this." He brushed a kiss across her forehead. "Or this." His lips tasted hers briefly once, twice, before he thrust her quickly away, holding her at arm's length.

Amy's eyelids fluttered, her body swaying from the suddenness of his onslaught and the shock of his withdrawal. Mike seemed determined to tease her with barely discernible caresses of his firm, gentle mouth.

She shook her head, blinking to clear her vision. "That's funny," she finally said with a tiny smile. "I was afraid you *wouldn't* kiss me again."

"I think we'd better go." Mike reached past her to pick up the pie and ice cream. "Before this melts."

"I had noticed it's awfully warm in here." She laughed nervously. "Must be a faulty thermostat. I'll have to have it checked."

Mike snorted. "Yeah. And it's getting worse by the minute." He held the door for her.

She let her gaze meet his. "Where to?"

Mike's voice sounded huskier than he wanted it to when he answered, "Your place."

Amy's apartment was the left half of a duplex on Calle El Segundo that had weathered the encroachment of the business district on the once-quiet, refined neighborhood. Evangeline Norton, a widow who minded everyone's business, peeked through her curtains as Amy's headlights illuminated both apartments. Out of habit and concern for the elderly woman's peace of mind, Amy waved to her.

Leaving room for Mike's Toyota, Amy purposely pulled the Jaguar to the upper end of her narrow driveway and watched him wheel expertly into place behind her.

He climbed out, balancing their dessert.

"Is it melted?" Amy called, waiting for him to join her.

"Nope. I drove with the windows open just for you."

Eyeing his wind-blown hair, she was not at all doubtful. She wanted to reach out and run her fingers through its thick, tumbled softness. His hair would be soft, she decided, and his skin would be warm with a masculinity that would make her want to touch and keep on touching.

Down, girl, Amy lectured herself. He's already let you know he doesn't want to get romantically involved. He's said he doesn't want to be tempted to kiss you. So be sensible. Stop fantasizing and behave yourself.

She chuckled as she led the way onto the porch and fitted her key into the lock. I'll be good, she promised. The door swung open. If, however, he manages to change his mind on his own, well, I won't be responsible.

Handing her the pie, he stepped into the living room. It was decorated in muted earth tones, the braided rug adding just enough color to the colonial furniture to make the whole effect one of welcoming warmth. A wing-backed couch stood near the wide front window, and matching chairs were grouped around it with a closeness that suggested intimate conversations as well as casual camaraderie. Mike felt instantly at home.

"The kitchen is through here," Amy said, tossing her purse next to the ruffled pillow on a deacon's bench. "Are you hungry?"

"I could eat."

"Good, because I missed dinner as usual," she called.

"Then you need more than dessert. It's not good for a person to live on sweets." Mike looked after her, then glanced around the room where she'd left him.

"Yes, *Daddy*," Amy shot back.

Something about her house had already given Mike a sense of déjà-vu. Before he could pinpoint the exact memory, Amy's reference to a parent made cold chills race up his back. That was it. The McPherson house. Sure. Alice and Tom and the two boys.

Mike gritted his teeth. He'd managed to stay with them nearly a year when he was—let's see—about nine, he guessed. Nice people. A family. Damn it all. For an instant he was a lonely child again, wondering why, in a world so filled with people, there was no special place meant just for him.

The gut reaction unsettled him, and he sought out Amy's company, Amy's smile.

"Hi. I missed you." She noticed he looked nervous, ill at ease.

Mike stuffed his hands into his pockets. "I missed you, too. You have a nice place here."

"Thanks. I'm about to cut the pie. How many wrinkles?"

"I beg your pardon?"

She laughed. "It's an old Alexander family joke. You look at the fluting of the pie crust, count the folds and tell me how many to count so I can cut a slice the size you want."

"Four, I guess." He had to walk away from her, from the idea of a happy family, from the pain the vision conjured up. "And one scoop of ice cream, if you please."

"I do please," Amy said, glancing over her shoulder as his voice drew farther away. "Go on back to the living room and make yourself comfortable. I'll join you as soon as I put a pot of coffee on to brew."

Amy pushed aside a package of frozen peas to make room for the remaining ice cream in her freezer. She could see Mike in the other room, running his fingers over the pillows on her couch, then pausing to stare at the family photographs hanging on the wall next to the bookcase. How pensive he seemed. How brooding. How lonely.

Not that she'd had all that much experience judging the inner workings of men's minds, Amy reminded herself. Still, there was something more bothering Mike than whether or not to kiss her again. His mood went deeper than the stirrings of affection they'd shared. And she was frightened for him.

Chapter Four

Working hard to display a cheerful expression Amy entered the living room bearing a tray with their desserts. She nodded toward the couch as she set the tray on her maple coffee table. "Here we are. Marino's finest."

Mike looked at her appreciatively, his eyes traveling slowly from her toes to the top of her head then settling on her face. "That's what I thought the minute I saw you there."

Amy blushed, less embarrassed than pleased. "Oh, you did?"

"I did." He edged closer to her as she sat down beside him. "And I haven't changed my mind."

Then why don't you want to kiss me? she wondered. Why do I keep getting such confusing messages from you? Amy chuckled. How on earth would she know if Mike was sending mixed signals? Her vast knowledge of men included her father, the poor janitor she'd had her childish crush on, several movie stars, one serious relationship in her senior year of high school that had broken up before much could come of it, and Mike Dixon. Not exactly a heavy track record.

She handed him one of the gold-bordered plates and a fork. "Four wrinkles. As ordered."

"Thanks." Mike tried not to flinch as she laid a napkin across his knee.

"You're welcome." Amy settled back. "Mind if I take my shoes off? My feet are killing me."

"No. Not at all. This is your house."

"But you're my guest," she reminded him. "I don't want to offend you."

"I doubt you could if you tried," Mike said, turning his attention to his pie and beginning to eat. Keep telling yourself this is *her* house, he prompted. No matter what it feels like, you don't belong here any more than you ever belonged in any of those other houses, and you know it.

Amy tucked her bare feet under her, picked up her plate and tasted the pie. It was good. Better than the look on Mike's sober face indicated.

He smiled halfheartedly. "As soon as we're done with this, let's dig into that stuff your parents left behind."

"There's no hurry."

Mike popped a bite of apple into his mouth.

"Yes, there is." He was certain the sooner he could make amends and distance himself from Amy and the attraction he felt toward her, the better off they'd *both* be. "Please?"

Without argument, she rose to fetch the box.

Empty dessert plates still sat on the maple table. The contents of a large cardboard box were spread on the rug, and Amy sat amidst the clutter, her legs folded, her attention fixed on the scrapbook in her lap. She turned a page.

"And here's the hospital where I was born," Amy said, pointing to the photograph of a matronly woman cradling a bundled baby.

Mike looked up from the yellowed newspaper clippings he'd been sorting through; Amy in the dress she'd sewed for her 4-H project, Amy placing second in a grade-school spelling bee, Amy's high-school graduation. "Is that your birth mother?" Mike's eyebrow arched.

"No. That's Mom. This is the page where I found her account of my adoption." Amy unfolded a piece of letter paper. "See?"

He took the paper from her and began to read. Martha Alexander was apparently explaining to no one in particular how she'd insisted on returning to the hospital where Amy had been born to have the photo taken. "Ray was furious when he found out, of course," Martha wrote. "But I had figured what he didn't know wouldn't hurt him, and I didn't see anything wrong with having a picture of the place to show to Amy, once she was older and could understand."

The page became a blur as Mike's mind wandered. Something *was* wrong here. What possible reason could Ray have had to be so set against letting his wife take an innocent picture? Mike couldn't put his finger on it, but something was very wrong.

Amy laid her hand on his arm. "Have you read, yet, where she says I'll understand when I'm older?"

"Huh? Oh, yes." Mike managed a brief smile for her benefit. "Her intentions were good. Apparently she just never got around to telling you."

Pensive, Amy stared at the photograph in the scrapbook. "Don't you think I could go to this hospital to trace my other mother?"

"Perhaps." His concentration wandered again to Martha's tightly drawn script as he looked for further clues. There were none. Still, even without a specific mention of location, it was obvious, from the sign on the hospital wall behind Martha and her baby, that the photo was of Mercy

Hospital in San Diego. "At least you have a city to start with."

She brightened. "That's what *I* thought. Isn't it wonderful?"

"Yeah. Great." San Diego. Mike puzzled a moment. He'd spent a little time working there after he got out of the army, but that wasn't what nagged at the fringes of his memory. What was it? What had he just seen that tied in with...?

Leaning forward, he began to rummage through the clutter on the floor. A full sheet of the San Diego *Herald* lay uncut amid the other papers. He'd thought it strange for a moment when he'd run across it, then put it out of his mind. Now he took a second look, and the headline sent chills up his spine. The date was right, the portent obvious.

Mike held his breath. He'd planned to give Amy the advice she needed then absent himself from her life before he got in too deeply. Now, he could see he'd made a serious error. He'd learned too much already to just walk out on her. She didn't know it yet, but she needed him.

Mike watched her as she smiled down on the collection of old photographs in the book. Amy Alexander was the dearest, most appealing woman he'd ever had the pleasure to meet. She was also one of the most vulnerable. Left to her own devices she was liable to stumble on information that would leave her profoundly and irrevocably hurt. Silently, Mike studied her enthusiastic expression. He mustn't let that happen, even if it meant he was the one who suffered instead.

Mike reached for the scrapbook and took it from her, closed it and placed it in the box atop the damning newspaper. "I want you to forget you were adopted," he said sternly, a catch in his throat. "Promise me."

"You know I can't do that." She put out her hands to reclaim the book. "It's not fair to ask."

Mike's hands closed over hers, stopping her. Think fast, Dixon. Now what? "If you really care what's fair, you'll remember how traumatic your sudden appearance might be to the woman who gave you up for adoption," he said.

Amy sighed. "Oh, is *that* what's been bothering you? Well, don't worry. All I want to know is where I came from and why. If my birth mother doesn't want contact with me I won't press it." She smiled at him. "I'd never purposely hurt anyone, Mike. You should know that."

"And what about you?" he asked. "What if you're the one who's hurt?"

She bowed her head, staring at the box that contained the records of her tenuous past. "I can take being hurt if that's how it has to be."

Mike released one of her hands and with two fingers gently lifted her chin. "But I don't know if I can stand watching that happen to you," he whispered. "I don't want it to. I won't let it."

Amy's lips parted, her eyes wide. "Plese, don't worry about me."

"I can't help myself." He sighed, feeling his self-control slowly slipping away. Resist, he ordered. Don't let her get to you.

But even as he cautioned himself, Mike realized it was too late. Amy had reached deep within and touched a tender part of him that he seldom acknowledged. It wasn't simply worry about her that was affecting him. It was more. Much more.

Slowly, as if watching someone else, Mike lowered his head and touched his lips to hers. The taste of vanilla and cinnamon lingered there, reminding him of the battle he'd fought and won watching her lick the ice cream off her fingers. Only this time their situation was different. This time they were alone, and she was too close, too appealing, too perfect to resist.

Mike deepened the kiss. Moving his lips softly over hers he explored the rapport of their heightened senses.

Amy made a faint, mewing sound, drawing herself up to meet him. This was as she had imagined his kiss could be, only better. Without his usual reserve, Mike Dixon was as intoxicating as a sip of champagne, as seductive as any hero she had ever read about. Her lips parted beneath his, and she heard him draw a shaky breath.

The rest of the clippings slipped onto the floor as he leaned over her, his persuasive ardor pulsing with an excitement that left her weak. When his arms encircled her, lifting her closer, Amy yielded, winding her arms around his waist. The muscles of his back rippled beneath her hands, and she could feel the hammering of his heart. She knew she was totally helpless to resist him—and it didn't surprise her one bit that she didn't care.

Mike sensed her surrender. She was so beautiful. And so innocent, he added cynically. What are you going to do, Dixon, ravage her and *then* tell her you can't continue seeing her? That you've never been able to settle down with anyone? Do you think this woman is the kind who can accept that?

He knew the answer was no. Amy might have a naturally captivating sexuality that surfaced when they were together, but she was definitely not the type who jumped from affair to affair, from man to man. Amy was steady. Serious. And he couldn't give her what she needed, what she deserved. He couldn't give her stability in a relationship, of that he was certain.

Slowly, reluctantly, Mike loosened his hold. When her eyelids fluttered open in wonder, he smiled tenderly.

"Mike?"

He shook his head, his breathing ragged, his loss of control an embarrassment to him. "I'm sorry, Amy. I have to be going."

"Why?" As her hands brushed across his shoulders for one last, fleeting caress, she knew her efforts were futile. It was plain from his expression that in his heart, Mike had already left her.

She watched as he got to his feet then accepted the hand he offered and let him help her up. "I don't understand," she said quietly. "Was it something I did?"

Averting his gaze he shook his head. "Not at all."

"Then what?"

"Look, I'm really sorry—about a lot of things." He lifted his eyes to meet hers and felt a stab of regret. She looked so lost, so confused. "Please," he begged. "Try to understand."

"I want to," she assured him. "Help me."

Mike laughed, and some of his tension dissipated. He managed a faint smile. "I *am* helping you, honey. I'm leaving."

"You could stay."

"No, I can't," he said firmly but gently. "I don't think you're ready for what might happen between us if I did."

He caressed her cheek. Stop this, his logical side ordered. The more affection you show her, the harder it will be on both of you.

Amy smiled, nestling her face in his palm for a second before he withdrew it. "I suppose you're right."

"You know I am." Backing away, he purposely stood apart from her.

As her emotions plummeted earthward Amy clasped her hands in front of her. Her knuckles whitened. "I hope you don't think too badly of me," she said softly. "I've always found it difficult to make friends—probably because my family moved so often—and I guess I just got carried away."

His expression told her Mike understood, so she went on. "When my father died I looked around me and I was alone. Not just minus a parent but truly alone. I'd lost touch with people I'd met growing up, and Mom and Dad had always

told me our family had no other members—no aunts,
uncles, cousins—you know." Amy tried to smile. "Do you
know how that aloneness frightened me?"

His voice was husky, low. "Yes."

Amy's eyes widened. "I'm not telling you all this to gain
your sympathy or convince you to stay. I just thought you
should know how I feel."

Mike's gut was wrenching, his heart split asunder. She
looked so small, so disarming, standing there pouring out
her soul to him. He wanted desperately to stop her—to quiet
her—before his own tenuous control snapped.

"What I'm trying to say is that I'm not usually such a
pushover." Amy blushed. "I don't regularly fall under a
man's spell and . . . well, you know."

"I know."

The small smile began to curl the corners of her mouth.
"If you know all that, then you must also know I really do
like you. I enjoy your company."

"I'm glad."

"Then we can still be friends?"

"Of course," Mike said. He wished with all his heart that
their friendship—or whatever she wanted to call it—would
last. But he knew better. Such relationships never worked
for him. Still, he reasoned no harm was done by letting Amy
assume it would this time.

Crouching, Mike began to straighten the mess on the
floor. "Let me help you with this before I go."

"I'll take care of it later. Leave it." Amy lifted his coat
from the back of her couch where he'd laid it and stroked
the smooth fabric before placing a hand lightly on his
shoulder. "Here. Don't forget your jacket."

"Thanks." Mike stood and slipped it on, grateful the diversion had given him time to think, to plan. "How about
a piece of Marino's apple pie to go?" he asked non-
chalantly.

Amy beamed happily, glad to be able to please him. "Sure. I'll get it." She paused halfway to the kitchen.

"I'll wait here."

She nodded.

As soon as she'd disappeared through the doorway, Mike began to sift through her memorabilia. Larger than the rest of the papers, the San Diego *Herald* page was easy to locate, but its size was also a drawback.

Mike folded it quickly, found it was still too large to cram into his inside jacket pocket and took it out to fold it over once more.

His hand was poised in the air with success a moment away when he saw Amy's return out of the corner of his eye.

Mike froze, motionless.

"Here you are!" she said gaily. "I gave you five wrinkles this time. One for the road."

Standing quite still, he waited for her to notice his transgression. She didn't seem to. The piece of pie was covered in clear plastic wrap and served on one of her fancy dessert plates.

She traded him the pie for the newspaper, tossing it absently into the box. "I told you I'd take care of that junk later. Don't fuss over it."

Feeling a sense of extreme relief Mike said, "Just trying to help." He eyed the pie. "Thanks."

"No problem. Besides," she added with a grin, "this way you have to bring my plate back."

"Crafty, aren't you?" There was no way he was going to be able to get his hands on the newspaper now. Not without inciting Amy's curiosity. She was too intelligent, too observant. If she hadn't been trusting, too, she'd already have suspected he was up to something.

Sure, he could look up the same issue in the archives and learn all he needed from it, but that would mean Amy was still in possession of the original. If only he could get her to promise she'd forget the box for a few months he'd have a chance of protecting her. As it was . . .

Amy smiled rather wickedly. "I have been known to be a bit sneaky at times, yes."

"Will you be home sometime tomorrow?" Mike asked, glancing at the delicate pink design on the plate. "It's a well-known fact that china plates should not be separated from their owners for more than a day or two at the most."

"Is that so?"

He traced an invisible X on his chest with one finger. "Cross my heart."

"Then we're in luck," Amy said. "Tomorrow is my day off. I'll be here all day, except for one quick trip to the market." Guilt at coercing him surfaced and she added, "Or you could drop the empty plate off at Marino's anytime you like."

"I'll bring it here." He had to. Otherwise, how could he gain access to the box of clippings? Suddenly serious, Mike touched her arm, feeling her shiver. "Promise me one thing?"

Amy was instantly in tune with his change of mood. "If I can."

"You can." His eyes darted to the box on the floor. "Promise you'll seal that up and not bother with it again until we can do it together?"

"Will we?" Amy was afraid to breathe, to move, to blink, for fear his answer would be delayed.

Taking a deep breath Mike nodded and kissed her on the forehead. "We will."

Amy followed quietly as he walked to the door. No further words were necessary. Mike would be coming back, and that was all that counted. If a magical genie had materialized offering to grant her one wish, one special dream, she wouldn't have chosen any differently.

Mike had a choice to make, visit Amy on her day off as he'd promised or beg off, make excuses and head for San

Diego to research her past. He'd made a shambles of his bedclothes by the time the morning sun topped the horizon, but at least he'd come up with a brilliant idea he was sure would permanently alleviate her loneliness.

He grinned and ran his fingers through his hair. There was no reason to rush to the newspaper archives to dig up dirt he didn't intend to share with Amy. And the new day would be the perfect time to implement his plan.

Throwing off the comforter and sheets, he swung his naked body out of bed, stretched, then strode across the beige carpet. He was a man in total charge of his life, a man who knows what he wants and sees that he gets it.

Only in this case, Mike predicted, heading for the shower, it was Amy Alexander's needs he was so certain about. He knew just what her situation lacked. A few phone calls and he'd be all set.

Amy's day dawned brightly. Sparrows twittered outside her bedroom window, beams of sunlight slipped across the hills outside to warm her through the lacy curtains, and the joy in her heart spilled over to color everything with beauty. The pale yellow of her bedroom walls looked more lustrous, the hues in her quilt were cheerful as never before, and the whole room had somehow expanded to accommodate her abounding delight with life.

It was cleaning and marketing day, usually her least favorite of the week, yet today nothing could spoil her happiness. Mike was coming. True, he hadn't said *when*, but he had made a point of asking if she was going to be home. For Amy, that was enough to base her dreams on. Enough to cause her mind to spin with lively melodies and tender love songs.

Standing beside her bed she quickly shed her short, gauzy nightgown. What a gorgeous day! How wonderful to be alive! She started to pull on the oversize pink sweatshirt and

pants she always wore when she cleaned her apartment, then
changed her mind. If Mike showed up early she didn't want
to get caught looking less than her best.

"We've agreed we're just friends," she argued to herself.
"What difference will it make if he sees me like that?"

Chuckling, Amy pulled open a dresser drawer and took
out her new jeans and the jewel-necked, blue and white an-
gora sweater she'd been saving for some unnamed special
occasion.

"Better. Much better," she mumbled, dressing quickly.
"No matter what time he comes I'll be ready." She pivoted
in front of the mirror above her dressing table, happy with
her image.

"Oh, yes," Amy drawled. "I certainly will be ready."

By eight o'clock that night Amy was past being ready for
anything, especially a visit from Mike Dixon. She'd spent
the entire day expecting his imminent arrival and been disappointed at every turn. Finally, she'd kicked off her shoes
and curled up on the couch to watch a movie on television.

It didn't help her mood that the film was an old romantic
comedy from the days when leading men were all suave and
handsome and heroines were enchantingly flighty. Now, if
real life was like that, Amy mused, then Mike would be here
beside me and I'd fall helplessly into his strong arms, easily
overlooking the fact I've wasted the entire day waiting for
him. She sighed. He wasn't coming, and that was that. It
was time she quit pretending he was.

Amy got to her feet and clicked off the TV. Enough was
enough. All that silly movie-style happiness was for fools,
anyway. Life wasn't like that. At least hers wasn't. She knew
that her current thoughts were self-defeating, yet at that
moment, in the solitude of her silent apartment, she
couldn't help entertaining a twinge of pity.

Do something, she demanded. Act, don't sit and brood.
Anything is better than feeling sorry for yourself.

Maybe a good, long run would lift her spirits, she reasoned. It usually did. Being on her high-school's track team had taught her the benefits of an exhilarating run, and she'd continued to jog for exercise and tension relief ever since. She wasn't a world-record beater, but that hardly mattered.

Changing into the pink sweats she'd rejected that morning, Amy removed her pearl earrings, tied a sweatband around her forehead and laced her running shoes. She tucked an extra house key into her pocket then went to the living room to do some warm-up stretches, switching on the stereo for musical accompaniment.

She was seated straddle-legged on the floor, reaching for her toes, when there was a knock on the door. Mrs. Norton, probably, Amy told herself. The stereo wasn't loud by Amy's standards, but good old Mrs. Norton could undoubtedly hear a mouse sneeze if it was three blocks away and sealed inside a bank vault! The trouble was, when Amy played music she liked to feel the vibrations, rattle a few windows.

"Sorry!" Amy called, lowering the volume. "I'll turn it off in a minute. I didn't mean to bother you."

"Meow."

Meow? Amy stared at the door as it creaked open, making a space barely five inches across. Through the opening crept an orange and white striped ball of fur with the biggest blue eyes Amy had ever seen. Tiny paws barely touched the floor, and the kitten was trembling.

"Aw. Here, baby." Amy reached to scoop it up as she flicked off the music. "Where did you come from?"

"The stork brought him." Mike's head poked through the doorway. "Can I come in, too?"

"No. I'm not dressed. Look at me."

"I am," Mike said, smiling at her. "You're cute."

"Cute? This kitten is cute. I don't want to be cute."

His warm and exuberant laugh filled the room. "That's a shame, because you're as cute as they come, Amy." He closed the door and crossed to perch on the edge of her couch, his elbows resting on his knees. "Almost as cute as Seymour."

"Seymour?" Amy was cradling the kitten close to her breast, and its quivering had been replaced by a rumbling purr she was certain Mrs. Norton could hear.

Raising the fur ball to eye level Amy smiled at its inquisitive expression. "This can't be a Seymour," she insisted. "It has to be a Fluffy or a Muffy or something like that."

"Nope." Mike was determined. "His name is Seymour. He told me so."

Eyes twinkling, Amy glanced at Mike. "*He* told you?"

"Sure did. We spent the day together, and he happened to mention it."

"Oh, he did, did he?"

"Uh-huh." Mike watched Amy's face. The gift of the kitten had pleased her, he knew, but there was still a certain reserve to her posture, her expression. She had expected his visit, had waited for him, and his lateness had disappointed her. He decided to explain.

"You see," Mike began, "it's only April."

Getting to her feet, Amy cuddled Seymour. "Have you been drinking, Mike Dixon?"

Mike held up his hands, palms toward her. "No. I swear. The problem is that even in the desert most domestic cats are just being born at this time of year." He smiled at Amy then let his gaze rest fondly on the kitten. "I had to drive nearly to Los Angeles to find one this age. That's why I'm so late."

"You *what*?"

"I said, I . . ."

"I heard what you said. Are you nuts?"

"Probably. Once I make up my mind to do something I usually find a way to follow through."

Crossing to Amy, Mike gently scratched behind Seymour's ears. "Anyway, coming from a city filled with alleys and roving tomcats, he couldn't be named Fluffy, could he? I mean, what would the neighbors say?"

"That's true." Light from the lamp fell across Mike's face, and Amy's attention was drawn once more to the shadow made by the scar on his left cheekbone. Was Mike also the product of a childhood in a rough neighborhood? she wondered. It might explain some of his confusing behavior.

"So, do you like him?" Mike was beaming at her and looking extremely pleased with himself.

"Me? He's mine?"

"As long as I have visitation rights," Mike said. He knew he was grinning stupidly at the picture of mutual affection Amy and the kitten portrayed and he didn't care. He'd given her exactly what he'd intended—a companion to love. Something most people needed—what Amy needed, whether she knew it or not.

Cynicism crept unbidden into his thoughts. At least the kitten would be faithful and not disappoint her. Amy could safely love it.

"What shall I feed him?" Amy glanced at the clock on the wall. "We'll have to find an all-night market and . . ."

"Whoa. Do you think I'd bring you a present without providing all he needs? Wait here."

In seconds Mike was back lugging a plastic litter box, a bag of cat litter and some food. "He should be hungry. I didn't dare feed him much on the trip home."

"Poor little guy," Amy crooned. "He must have been terrified to ride all that way in the car."

Mike carried the paraphernalia into the kitchen and set it on the floor. "Oh, I wouldn't say that. He spent the afternoon curled up in my lap."

I'd be happy spending the day curled up in your lap, Amy thought. I'd be happy anywhere around you. She took two plastic bowls from the cupboard and watched Mike fill one with fresh water then place it on the floor. "Should we soak his food?"

Mike shrugged. "Beats me. I never had a pet of my own. The pet-shop lady said this stuff was what we needed, though." He ripped open a corner of the bag and scooped a handful of the pinkish-brown pellets into the other bowl. "Put him down and let's see what he does."

Surprised by Mike's admission, Amy asked, "You didn't?"

"Didn't what?" He was watching Seymour sneak up on his food dish.

"Have a pet. I grew up thinking I was the only kid in the world who couldn't have a pet of my own. We moved around so much my parents said it would be impossible."

She smiled wistfully at Mike, her eyes misty. Resting her palms on his chest, she impulsively kissed him on the cheek. "I've always wanted a kitten. Thank you, Mike."

"You're welcome." Turning away, Mike busied himself setting up the litter box on her service porch while he carefully avoided looking at Amy. It was enough that she was pleased with his gift. He didn't want sloppy displays of gratitude *or* her pity for any imagined lack in his childhood. It was Amy who needed the company of a pet; not him. He was doing just fine alone. And he didn't need to feel so damned protective toward her, either. Now, all he had to do was figure out how to stop.

She came up behind him. "Did you move a lot, too?"

There it was. The first of many questions to come if he didn't get away from her. Mike tensed. "Yeah. I moved."

"You mean your family moved. That's rough on kids, isn't it?"

He felt her light touch on his shoulder and made the mistake of glancing at her. "I suppose so."

For a fleeting moment Mike was six years old again, coming home from school to a houseful of police and firemen and knowing they had to have come to take care of his mother.

He'd run screaming for her, but a burly police officer had grabbed him and carried him outside before he could get to her bedroom. He'd kicked and punched and sobbed but it had done him no good.

They didn't even let him tell her goodbye.

Chapter Five

Amy stared. Mike's rugged countenance had undergone a transition she wouldn't have believed if she hadn't seen it happening. For a few moments there had been a softening of his expression, then he'd been overcome by a look of dread and apprehensiveness that reached into her core and made her ache for him. His eyes were moist, his jaw set yet trembling just a fraction.

With his hair falling in a wave across his forehead, his gaze blank and unfocused, it was as if he was a different person—no less a man and yet a gentler, more vulnerable soul. She wanted to reach out and hug him until whatever ghost was haunting him was exorcised for good.

"Mike?" Her voice was a whisper. "Are you all right?"

He shook himself, blinking to clear his vision, and stood rigidly erect. "Of course."

Amy laid one hand on his arm. "Really?"

"I told you, I'm fine." He started to walk away. "Look, you and Seymour need to get used to each other, and I've had a long day. I'd better be going."

"Must you? I mean . . . you just got here."

"You need your rest," he said.

"I need the company more," Amy confessed quietly. "There's a good movie on television, and I'm loaded with microwave popcorn." When he seemed unwilling or unable to decide she added, "How about it?"

Instinct told Mike to leave the peaceful sanctuary she offered, but he chose not to listen to the murmurs of his inner self. It would be good to spend more time with Amy. In her presence, in her house, he felt wanted, comfortable.

That's a dangerous attitude, Dixon, he warned. The woman is too good to be true. No one is that concerned, that caring, that real. Situations like this just don't happen—at least not to you.

But why not stay? he countered. I must be entitled to some pleasures other than what I'm able to provide for myself. Mike laughed at his ridiculous attitude. He was entitled to nothing, to no one special. If he'd learned anything in his sobering childhood, it was that truth. End of argument.

Still, he thought, recognizing his mind's feeble attempts to rationalize, and accepting them, staying with Amy might afford him another chance to pilfer the newspaper he'd tried to nab before.

Amy could see the battle Mike was waging with himself. When a halfhearted smile began to tug at the corners of his firm mouth, she knew she'd won.

"Good!" she said, not waiting for him to confirm the message she'd read in his expression. "I'll start the popcorn."

"I never said—"

"Sure, you did." Amy plopped Seymour into his litter box on her way to the pantry. "I distinctly remember reading your mind."

Mike's smile grew. She was quite a lady, this Amy Alexander, able to accept his obvious hesitancy and make it into a lighthearted cause for celebration. "Is mind reading one of your hidden talents?"

"Uh-huh. Maybe I'm the long-lost offspring of a traveling gypsy maiden. Who knows?"

He was chuckling. "Okay. You've convinced me. I'll stay."

"I knew you would," Amy fibbed, glad she'd followed her hunch and spoken out. She unfolded the compressed popcorn bag, put it in the microwave oven, set the dials on the oven and shut the door to start the cooking.

"You're pretty sure of yourself, aren't you?"

"Usually." She shot a brilliant smile his way. "While I watch this, how about getting a couple of sodas out of the refrigerator?"

"You're giving me refrigerator privileges, too?" Mike quipped. "Where will this all end?"

"With two friends spending a nice, quiet evening together in front of the TV," she warned. "Just for the record, I was *not* propositioning you when I asked you to stay."

"You weren't?" Lord, she was an appealing woman, so righteously indignant looking with her hands on her hips and her chin thrust out at him.

"No, I wasn't." As much as Amy wanted to be in Mike's arms, immersed in the wonder of his kisses, she knew that this was not the time. First Mike needed a friend. Whatever else developed between them would have to wait. There would be time, later, for the physical closeness she craved with him.

Don't think about what might come later, Amy lectured herself. Concentrate on the present. Mike isn't the only one who needs a friend, and you certainly could do worse. But you could never do better, she concluded. There was no one else she'd rather be with, rather confide in, than Mike Dixon.

"All right." Smiling, he peered into the refrigerator. "Cola or root beer?"

"Cola," Amy answered. "Sorry I don't have anything stronger."

"No problem." He straightened with two cans in his hands. "Besides, I wouldn't want you to get me drunk and try to take advantage of me."

"Ha! Fat chance. Don't you trust me?"

"Sure, I trust you, Ms. Alexander," he drawled.

"Good." The bell on her microwave oven sounded, and Amy withdrew the puffy white bag of steaming popcorn. "Um. Now it even *smells* like the movies. Come on. I want to see Cary Grant get the girl."

Silently, Mike followed her into the living room, sat beside her on the couch and accepted the popcorn she offered. But he found he could hardly swallow it. His throat had constricted, and his pulse was thudding in his temples. It had all started a few minutes ago when he'd realized he'd spoken the truth. He *did* trust Amy.

For longer than he could remember he'd made his way through life cautiously, relying on no one but himself. He didn't know how Amy had done it, but she'd broken through his guard.

Beyond a doubt, he truly wanted to stay.

Amy's feet were curled under her. She was finishing their second bag of popcorn by the time the movie ended.

She stretched. "Wasn't that wonderful?" Sighing, she reached for the remote control. "Want to watch the news?"

Rather than an answer from Mike, she heard an unmistakable snore.

Amy's head snapped around. He was asleep! Some interesting companion *she'd* turned out to be.

Her heart turned flip-flops, and she couldn't help but smile down at him. He looked positively endearing leaning there, his arms folded across his chest, his feet propped on the coffee table.

Mike's head had fallen back, and his lips were slightly parted. It took monumental restraint on Amy's part to keep from leaning over to kiss him as she brushed his arm with her hand.

Her voice was softly coaxing. "Mike? Yoo-hoo?"

He didn't stir. Well, you promised him an evening of two friends just relaxing together, she told herself. His lethargic state proved that.

Amy let her hand stroke his arm. Her caress, meant to awaken him, was also a gentle affirmation of the acceptance she wanted him to feel.

"Mike? Mike? The movie's over," she said a little louder than before.

She sighed. Deciding to leave him alone, she withdrew. He deserved to sleep after driving all that way to bring her the kitten. And it was evident the evening spent with her had done him some good, too. He'd finally relaxed, eliminating the stress lines in his forehead and the small creases around his eyes.

The tiny, crescent-shaped scar was still evident on his cheek, though, the only visible remnant of the rough life Amy was now fairly certain he had lived. If he would only open up to her, if only he *could*, she was positive he'd feel better. And she would be better equipped to deal with whatever it was that made him continually withdraw from her arms just when she was beginning to enjoy their closeness the most.

Amy flushed, an unsettling warmth coursing through her veins. Mike looked so appealing, so desirable, lying there. Her heart joined the chorus her body was singing...so easy to love.

Her breathing stopped, her eyes widening.

"Love?" she whispered.

With a groan, Amy nodded, drawing her knees up under her chin. Oh, yes. Love. She'd managed to push aside her serious thoughts about Mike for long enough. It was time she admitted the depth of her feelings. Mike Dixon might not be aware of it—might not be ready to accept it—but Amy was already falling irrevocably in love with him.

Now what? she asked herself. Now, nothing, came the answer. You promised him a friend and that's what he'll get until he's ready to ask for more. Just back off and bide your time. He'll come around.

Lots of luck, Amy, her heart taunted. You may be patient, but everyone has limits. You're going to wait and give him no sign you wish there were more between the two of you? Ha! *This*, I've got to see.

When she draped an afghan around him, Mike settled even deeper into the couch. Seymour had followed Amy from the bedroom, spotted Mike and curled up beside him.

"Okay," she whispered, ruffling the fur between the kitten's ears, "you two boys get some sleep, and I'll wake you in the morning."

It was Seymour's answering meow, that finally woke Mike.

His eyes opened slowly at first, as if he didn't believe what he was seeing. The corners of his mouth lifted as he focused on Amy's face, and she could have sworn she read affection in his expression. Then, in an instant, Mike remembered where he was and everything changed.

"Hey!" Straightening, he nearly dumped the kitten on the floor.

"Careful!" Amy scooped up her new pet.

"What's going on here?"

Scowling, she faced Mike. "You don't have to get upset. I tried to wake you."

"You couldn't have. I'm a very light sleeper. I'd have heard you."

He pushed aside the blanket and got to his feet. Running his fingers through his hair, he forced his eyes to open and stay that way. For a second he'd felt the same calmness and relief he sometimes experienced after making love to a woman. Only this time, all he'd had to do was wake up to the vision of Amy's kindhearted face! He was in trouble all right. Deep trouble.

"Well, I *did* try," she insisted. "You were practically unconscious, you were sleeping so soundly."

"That's impossible," Mike argued. Out of control of both the situation and his feelings for Amy, he knew he had to pull himself together and get the hell away from her before he did something even *more* stupid than falling asleep.

Blushing slightly, Mike shook his head. "Okay. I'm sorry."

"For what?"

The color creeping up his neck deepened. The omissions for which he was truly sorry were *not* the kinds of things he could share with someone as innocent as Amy.

"For doubting you and for conking out like that," Mike said. "Some brilliant conversationalist, huh?"

"I didn't mind. Really." Her smile was genuinely forgiving. "I enjoyed having you here."

Chuckling, Mike nodded. "Oh, sure."

"Honestly, I did." Her voice lowered. "You don't have to entertain me to make me like having you around. It's enough to just be there."

"Is it?" Touched by Amy's frankness, Mike had to close the distance between them in spite of the promises he'd made to himself. When he stopped, only the presence of Seymour in Amy's arms kept their bodies apart.

She lowered her eyes, releasing the kitten onto the couch then looking up into Mike's darkening gaze. "You know how it is."

"Yes," he said. "I do know."

Amy closed her eyes, swaying against him, as his mouth descended to claim hers. This time his kiss lingered, his lips pressing harder, demanding she respond. And when she did the husky groan that rumbled in Mike's throat reached into her own core and knotted into a pleasurable ache she found unfathomable. Standing on tiptoe, she met his onslaught of her senses with a force and need that shocked yet thrilled her.

Entwining her arms around his neck, Amy edged closer, wanting to become a part of every inch of him, to touch and be touched until there was nothing left but the two of them, lost together in the mindless longing that was consuming her. This was what she'd dreamed of. This was what she'd been born for. It no longer mattered why she had come to this moment in time, or what path had brought her. Nothing counted but the marvelous man in whose arms she languished. There was no yesterday, no present except what was happening in her heart, in her body.

Leaving her lips, Mike trailed kisses across her cheek and down her neck as his hands roamed restlessly over her back. Burying his face in the softness of her shoulder, he moaned, then threw his head back and pulled her so close Amy could hardly breathe. She saw his jaw clench.

Amy's hands explored the warm expanse of Mike's chest, and the pounding beat of his heart beneath her fingertips told her all she needed to know. Without her conscious command her body moved against him, her hips settling into the curves of his until they fit perfectly.

Mike's breathing was ragged as he lowered his gaze and filled his hand with the silk of her hair. "No, Amy, don't. Please."

She was loathe to let him move away, and she slid her arms around his waist and held him tightly, further intensifying the ache of passion they shared.

He thrust her away, cupping her face in his hands and forcing her to look at him. "Forgive me, Amy. I didn't mean to kiss you that way. When I woke up and you were standing there, so beautiful, so desirable, I guess it affected me more strongly than I thought. I'm sorry."

She laid her fingertips across his lips, feeling dizzy when he kissed them, too. "Don't apologize. You knew what I wanted."

"Yes." He kissed her forehead. "But I'm the one responsible. I was thoroughly aware of what would happen if I touched you again. And I did it anyway."

"I knew, too," she said softly.

"Did you?" He barely smiled. "I wonder." Amy's eyes were bright with longing, her lips slightly parted. Mike's already taut body screamed for release against the constraints of his conscience. But not like this, he lamented. Not at Amy's expense.

He had to ask, "How many men have you had, Amy? One? Two?"

"I don't see..." Suddenly she was nervous. It was as if he expected her to be experienced and would be disappointed to learn she wasn't.

"That's what I thought," Mike said tenderly. "And your first lover should be someone special."

"Someone like you," she suggested, half holding her breath.

Mike released her and stepped away. "No. Not like me. Not ever like me. Don't wish that on yourself, Amy."

But she did. Heaven help her, she did. Her arms reached after him, her body clinging to the sensations he had kindled in her.

When Mike acted as if she wasn't even there, Amy let her arms fall to her sides and watched him pull on his jacket as he walked to the door. Turn around! her heart shouted. Don't go! Don't you know I *love* you?

He did try to smile as he glanced at her, but the effect was one of sadness, not joy. "Good night."

Afraid that if she spoke she would say something she would ultimately regret, Amy only nodded.

When she heard his car start and the sound of the engine fade into the distance she picked up Seymour and held him close.

"Damn. Why does he always *leave* me just when things are getting interesting?" she demanded, placing a conciliatory kiss on the top of Seymour's head.

The kitten's front feet pushed alternately against her arm, his claws kneading but not hurting.

"You miss your mama, don't you, baby?" she crooned, holding him closer. "Well, I miss mine, too."

Squaring her shoulders, Amy started for the kitchen. "How about a bowl of warm milk, huh?"

Seymour purred.

"That's what I thought. Warm milk will fix you right up, and you can go to sleep and dream of the most wonderful things, like climbing trees and playing hide-and-seek with your brothers and sisters, and—"

She stopped her chattering and stared deeply into the trusting, inquisitive blue eyes. "Never mind, Seymour. I'm being silly. You can't go back, you know. None of us can."

But we can go forward, go on with our lives, her heart reminded her. We can play with the cards fate has dealt us and make the best of things.

And sometimes that means we have to gamble, she added, on ourselves *and* on other people. On people like her birth parents. On people like Mike Dixon.

Amy smiled. Mike was worth taking a chance on the same way her parents had gambled on her when they'd taken a stranger's baby into their home and their hearts.

She laughed aloud, startling Seymour, so she smoothly stroked his fur to quiet him.

"I sound like I'm about to *adopt* Mike," she said to the raptly attentive kitten. "And that, little one, is not what I had in mind. Not at all."

* * *

Two evenings passed before Amy saw Mike enter Marino's again. He was dressed more casually than usual in a plain tan sweater and jeans. His hair was mussed, his face shadowed by the beginnings of a beard.

The joy in Amy's heart when she glimpsed his welcome smile was almost too sweet to bear. "Hello!"

"Hi." Mike's thumbs were hooked into the front pockets of his jeans, his stance deceptively nonchalant. "I thought I should check up on Seymour."

"He asks about you," she said.

"He does, huh? I thought he might. We were pretty close."

"That's what he told me."

"What else did he tell you?" Mike was leaning against the counter, glancing lazily at the silk fabric that covered her, yet revealed.

Amy busied herself at the cash register and tried not to blush at his open admiration. "Seymour reminded me you promised to visit him."

"Parents don't always keep their promises," Mike said, a bit more cynically than he'd intended.

"Mine did." Amy's smile was tender, understanding.

"Yeah. Well, I've been meaning to discuss something with you, and I guess now's as good a time as any."

She hesitated to comment, unsure whether he was still teasing or actually as serious as he sounded. "Okay."

Mike carefully looked away, perusing the colors in the stained-glass window. "I want you to give me the box of stuff your parents left."

"That's silly. Why would I want to do that?"

"To ease your mind?" He turned to her and shrugged. "Maybe to remove the temptation to dig through it some more? I don't know."

Amy shook her head. "No."

"No what?"

"No dice, Mike." She shot him an easy grin. "As a matter of fact, I came to a decision the other night after you left."

He straightened. "Oh?"

"Uh-huh. I've been acting childishly melodramatic about the whole situation."

Tensing, Mike fought to maintain his casual air. "Go on."

"There's not much to say except that I've decided to make a few inquiries on my own, and if nothing comes of them I'll drop the whole idea."

He leaned forward, his hand closing on her wrist. He couldn't let her delve into her past. Not considering what he'd just learned. "Drop it, please," he begged. "Before you begin."

Amy twisted free. "Don't be silly. And don't worry. I won't show up on some poor woman's doorstep and ruin her life. I swear."

"No. You can't pursue this."

"Of course, I can. All I have to do is visit the hospital and make some discreet inquiries. That can't hurt."

"Amy—"

Marissa appeared at her elbow. "I hate to interrupt but Alonzo's on the warpath again."

"It's okay." Smiling at Mike to reassure him, Amy came out from behind the counter. "Would you like to visit Seymour tonight?" She held her breath, hoping he'd agree.

Would he like to visit again? Not exactly, Mike thought. What he would like to do is kidnap Amy and carry her off to some safe place where reality could never reach her.

He put an end to the lunatic meanderings of his mind by asking, "When do you get off work?"

Amy's breath left her in an audible whoosh but Mike seemed to take no notice of it. "I'm through at nine tonight, but Seymour would probably like some company before that.'' Amy giggled. ''Yesterday, he got bored and unrolled an entire roll of toilet paper all over the floor.''

''Smart kitty.''

''Too smart.'' It took her only seconds to decide what to say next. ''You'll find a key in the flowerpot by the kitchen door. Why don't you go to my place early and try to prevent further mayhem?''

Mike couldn't believe his stroke of luck! He'd spent every minute since his trip to the newspaper archives trying to figure out how he was going to get into Amy's apartment without her, short of breaking and entering, never dreaming she'd simply invite him.

He smiled, his stiff posture relaxing, and ran his hand over the dark stubble on his chin. ''That sounds like a good plan, only first I need to go home, shower and shave. The last couple of days have been pretty rough.''

''I had noticed,'' Amy said dryly. ''It must be the weather. Make yourself at home when you get to the house and kiss Seymour for me, okay?''

''How about I skip kissing the cat and just fix you some dinner while I wait?''

''That may be harder to do than you think,'' she said.

''I doubt it. Seymour's not my type.''

''Not *that*, the dinner,'' Amy countered, chuckling and shaking her head. ''I missed my usual trip to the market this week, and the pantry is pretty bare.''

''I'll find something,'' Mike said. ''See you after nine?''

''That sounds wonderful.'' Amy paused, hating to bid him goodbye. He was smiling broadly, and she should have been able to accept the validity of his expression, yet she couldn't. The open, guileless grin she'd come to associate with Mike in his more unguarded moments wasn't what he wore on his face now. Instead, his eyes betrayed something deeper, as if a part of him was being purposely withheld, kept secret.

You're imagining things, Amy told herself. He's here, isn't he? He came even after he'd been so insistent that he was wrong for you. Accept it. Accept him. And for goodness sake, quit questioning your blessings!

Mike started for the door. "Count on dinner, lady. And don't worry about Seymour. I'll baby-sit him for you."

She waved, grinning so broadly her cheeks hurt as he ducked out the door. A constriction squeezed her chest, and she recognized at once that seeing Mike leave had caused the reaction. He was already so dear, so important to her, that it hurt to be away from him.

Resting her fingertips against her lips, Amy stood alone amid the bustle of the busy restaurant. Mike couldn't have meant what he'd said the other night about not wanting to be her lover. He couldn't have…because if he did, she knew she was going to ache for him for the rest of her life. Maybe longer.

Chapter Six

True to his promise, Mike had dinner waiting when Amy burst breathlessly into the house at ten minutes after nine. She slipped her shoes off in the entry and padded quietly to the kitchen, drawn by the pungent aroma of spices and the certainty she'd find Mike there.

His back was to her, and she delayed making her presence known long enough to drink in the marvelous sight of him. He'd changed into a chambray shirt and he had the sleeves rolled up, baring the fine hairs on his forearms. He leaned over an iron kettle on her stove and lifted a wooden spoon to his lips.

A shiver of delight traveled from Amy's head to her toes and back again. Mike and Seymour noticed her at the same time. She smiled, bending low to run her hand over the kitten's back. "Hello. Have you been good?"

"I don't know about him," Mike said, "but I've been behaving myself." He cocked his head toward the stove. "Come see."

Crossing to him, she leaned over and drew a deep breath. "That smells wonderful. What is it?"

"Mulligan stew," he said. "I picked up the meat and vegetables on the way over, but you had the rest of the ingredients."

"What else is in it?" If Mike liked it, she'd have to learn to make it for him.

"Water and spices." Mike laughed, shouldered her aside and ladled a bowl full. "I built a fire in the fireplace. Why don't you eat in the living room and enjoy it?"

Amy followed his lead. "That sounds heavenly. A fire is just what I need to relax."

"It was sure what *I* needed," Mike muttered. "You have no idea how relaxed I feel since I lit it."

Plopping down on the couch, Amy accepted the bowl of stew then looked questioningly at Mike. "Where's yours?"

"Sorry. I have to go." He was already heading for the door. "I put your key back in the flowerpot."

"You're leaving? But—"

"I have a wandering husband to watch tonight. His wife doubts he plays poker with the guys five evenings a week."

"Does he?" It was the first time Mike had mentioned his work, and Amy was interested.

"Probably not. However, we can always hope."

Setting aside the bowl and spoon, Amy joined him at the door. "I really didn't mean to keep you from doing your job. I'm sorry."

"Don't worry about it," Mike said. "I don't feel like I wasted my time by coming here. After all, I got to play with Seymour."

"That's right," she agreed, glancing around the room. "Now where did he disappear to?"

"He's in the kitchen, eating his dinner like a good boy, which is what *you* should be doing." Mike turned her forcibly and gave her an easy push toward the couch.

"I'm going. I'm going." Amy looked at him. "Will I see you again?" Subtle, Amy. She grimaced. Real subtle. Congratulations on your tact and cautious approach.

"Visitation rights, remember?"

What the heck, she'd already let him know how she felt, how much she wanted to see him again. There was no sense pretending to be coy. "Soon?"

"Sure," he said. "When I can."

Mike's idea of soon and hers obviously differed, Amy thought, pacing aimlessly. In desperation, she headed for her bedroom and the box stored there.

It wasn't that she relished going against what Mike had asked of her regarding her adoption. But her days had been so empty since the last time she'd seen him that her mind needed something less personally destructive on which to focus.

Perhaps if she sorted and catalogued her father's papers she'd see a clearer path to finding her birth parents, she reasoned. Anyway, it beat sitting around waiting for the phone to ring.

Seymour helped. Batting loose papers across the rug and then chasing them, he managed to lengthen what should have been a two-hour job into one that took much longer. Growing noticeably larger almost daily, the naughty kitten was now capable of considerably more mayhem than he had been when he fit snugly in the palm of Mike's hand.

Sighing, Amy banished remembrances of Mike from her mind, put a rubber band around the last bunch of letters and laid the packet in the box. A rattling, crinkling sound under her couch led her to get down on her knees to peek. Seymour was putting a series of tooth-sized perforations in another piece of newspaper. Not yellowed, the paper was obviously a current one.

Ignoring his harmless fetish, Amy left him alone and stood, rubbing the knotted muscles in her neck. At first she'd thought the mischievous cat had made off with the largest piece of paper in the box, but luckily he'd chosen a recent daily.

Amy stood very still, scowling. In that case, where was the big sheet of paper she remembered seeing in with the rest? Surely, she would have noticed Seymour dragging off something as large as that. She scanned the floor and the bundles in the box. It hadn't been overlooked. It simply wasn't there.

Deep in thought, Amy wandered to the kitchen, got a soda out of the refrigerator and popped the top. The spritzing sound brought the kitten on the run.

"Where is it, baby?" Amy asked him. "You wouldn't be holding out on me, would you?"

"Mrrow."

"That's what I thought. Okay. I believe you." Her mind tumbled the question around and around. Where was the silly thing?

Wandering into the living room she settled herself on the couch with Seymour in her lap. She hadn't intended to bother reading most of the dull clippings collection, but now her curiosity was piqued. Maybe fate was trying to tell her something by causing her to misplace the largest sheet of paper. Perhaps a clue in the *other* clippings was what she really needed to see.

Settling herself on the couch, she hefted the box. She had nothing to lose but time, and lately she'd had an abundance of that. Darn it.

Ruffling the kitten's ears, Amy began to read.

The telephone rang three times before anyone at the police department answered. Amy gripped the receiver in one hand, an old piece of newsprint clutched in the other, as a man's deep voice greeted her with, "Lieutenant Finch."

"Hello." Amy wasn't quite sure how to begin without sounding crazy. She checked the name on the clipping. "I wonder if I might speak to Lieutenant Tim O'Neil, please?"

There was a momentary silence on the line. "O'Neil is no longer with us, ma'am. He retired. Can I help you?"

Amy peered at the yellowed newspaper article. She'd given the right name, and the telephone number asking for the public's help was obviously still that of the San Diego Police Department, but since O'Neil had retired she supposed it was foolish to expect to be able to learn anything pertinent.

She plunged ahead anyway. "Thanks. I doubt you can do much for me at this late date. You see, I'm researching a case Lieutenant O'Neil was involved in over twenty years ago, and I wanted to ask him some questions."

Finch was polite. "I'm sorry, ma'am. O'Neil isn't here anymore."

"I'm sorry to have bothered you," Amy said.

"It's no bother," he said. "Public relations is just part of my job."

"I see." Amy was thoughtful. "Then maybe you can suggest another way of approaching my problem. I mean, there must be some alternative."

"Perhaps. There are always the newspaper accounts, only we all know how those can get distorted. Listen, I've been around here a while, myself. If the case you're interested in was important at the time, I might remember something that would help you."

Suddenly nervous at the prospect of a clue—any clue—Amy swallowed to relieve the dryness in her throat. "It's the case with all the missing babies," she said. Her voice had begun to sound foreign to her, and she had to sit down.

"Oh, *that* one." Finch paused. "And how is the weather in the desert today?"

"Fine, but—" Confused, Amy fell silent.

"That's what I thought. You wouldn't happen to be working with a certain investigator from Search International in Palm Springs, would you?"

"Mike?"

"Yeah, Mike Dixon." The lieutenant chuckled. "Well, you can tell him he got all the information out of me he's gonna get when he was down here last week. You understand?"

"But—"

"No buts, lady. I got my tail in a wringer for telling him as much as I did, even if it was off the record. He should know better than to try to get to me through a woman."

There was a click as the line went dead.

Amy sat perfectly still, the breath coursing in and out of her lungs the only perceptible movement in the room.

Sensitive to her mood, Seymour crept out from under the couch and cautiously began to rub against her leg. "Meow?"

"He lied," Amy muttered. Her voice grew louder. "He *lied* to me!"

The kitten stopped moving and stared. Amy met his inquisitive gaze, reached down and lifted him into her arms. "Come here, baby. I'm sorry if I scared you."

It was soothing to cuddle the warmly affectionate creature, and his purring made her feel cherished, accepted. She kissed him on the top of the head to reassure him, and Seymour obligingly snuggled closer.

"Your friend Mike has been a busy boy," she confided to the kitten. "Did you know he's been working on my case behind my back?"

"Meow?"

"That's right. He has." She got to her feet, carrying Seymour with her to the window. Sighing, she stared at the passing traffic. In less than an hour she was due at Marino's. And once at work, she might not be able to get away until long after Search International had closed for the day. That would mean it might be days before she managed to track Mike down and confront him. No. Work or no work, she had to know what was going on, and *soon*.

Lowering Seymour to the couch, Amy punched Marino's familiar number into her telephone. Marissa answered.

"I may be a few minutes late," Amy told her. "Can you handle things till I get there?"

"Sure. Are you okay? You sound funny."

"I'm fine. Just peachy," Amy said. "Hold the fort for me, and I'll fill you in later."

"Okay. Take all the time you need."

"Thanks." Having made up her mind what she had to do, the rest was easy. Her first reaction had been stunned silence, then a feeling of betrayal. And now? Amy searched her heart for more excuses to overlook Mike's deceptions and found none she could accept. She was angry and in no mood to fight it. She was, however, in a fine mood to face Mike Dixon.

"And don't worry," Amy said icily. "I have a feeling my errand won't take long at all."

"Ooh. Sounds serious."

"It is," Amy assured her. "You have no idea how serious."

"You promise I'll hear all the juicy details eventually?"

"Sure." Amy's chuckle was more sardonic than humorous. "I know I'll need someone who's a good listener when this is all over."

"Hey. No sweat. What are friends for?"

"That's part of the problem," Amy admitted ruefully. "I thought I knew and I was oh, so wrong."

Amy had never dressed for work as quickly as she did that day. A breeze out of the north had put a chill in the air so she pulled a bright pink sweater over her blouse, flouncing the white silk bow at her throat through the sweater's V neck. The effect was striking. And so it should be, she maintained, adding pearl earrings. Mike deserved to see her looking her best when she . . .

When she what? Certainly her anger over his deceptions was valid. Yet perhaps he felt he had good reason to hide the truth from her. Perhaps he was deluded rather than deceitful. He did deserve a chance to explain. One chance. Period. And his excuses had better be good.

Amy made sure Seymour had fresh food and water, closed her bedroom door to keep him out of the basket of clean laundry she hadn't taken the time to put away, shouldered her purse and stepped outside. Today, she'd walk. It wasn't that far from her house to Mike's office and as upset as she was, she didn't trust herself behind the wheel of a car.

Striding briskly, Amy rehearsed their forthcoming meeting. She'd confront him with what she'd learned and insist he tell her the rest. That wasn't so much to ask. Not since he'd chosen to keep *everything* from her. Not since he'd deliberately lied!

Normally, her brisk walk would have calmed Amy's nerves, but today her mind was so busy that she arrived at Search International in a state of mental chaos. It never occurred to her that Mike might be with another client when she rushed past his surprised secretary and burst into his office unannounced. Luckily he was alone.

Getting to his feet, Mike waved to the concerned secretary who had pursued Amy through the door. "It's all right, Marie. I can handle this." As she backed out the door, he added, "Hold my calls."

Mike moved slowly because of Amy's visibly agitated state. He didn't try to approach or touch her. Instead he gestured to a chair opposite his desk. "Won't you have a seat?"

"No. I will not." Disgusted with herself for being able to display so little self-control, Amy paced to the window and back.

"I was going to call you," he said quietly.

Her mouth dropped open and she snapped it shut. "Call me? You think I'm here because you didn't *call* me?"

"Then why?"

"Does the name Tim O'Neil sound familiar?" Very little changed in Mike's concerned expression, yet Amy was certain she detected a slight flinch, a tightening of his muscles. When Mike hesitated to answer, she added, "And don't lie to me. Not again."

He arched his eyebrows. "I didn't lie to you, Amy."

"Oh, no? Then why did Lieutenant Finch of the San Diego police department say he was in trouble because of something he'd told you?" She waited. "Well?"

"Well, nothing." Shrugging, Mike sat down behind his desk and leaned back, the picture of studied ease. "I used to do some free-lance work for San Diego and I sometimes worked with Finch. That's all."

Amy clenched her hands together. "No, Mike, that's not all. What about the missing babies?" There it was again. She was certain she'd seen it this time. Mike's supposedly relaxed body had given an involuntary jerk, and his eyes had widened just enough for her to be sure he was withholding information.

"I don't know what you mean."

"Oh, Mike." Her voice was pleading now. "Don't do this to me. I thought we were friends. I *trusted* you."

"Amy..." Rising, he stepped around the desk to her.

"No. Don't touch me. Just talk to me." She held up her hands to ward him off, but the gesture wasn't necessary. Mike kept his distance.

"There's nothing to talk about," he insisted. "You're overwrought and imagining things."

"Am I imagining the clipping?"

Mike's head snapped around. "Clipping? What clipping? What are you saying?"

"It was such a little thing," she declared thoughtfully. "I'd almost given up finding any new data when I saw this among Dad's old newspaper clippings." She pulled a crumpled piece of paper out of her purse and held it up briefly for him to see. "I don't know why he would have saved it unless..."

Amy's anger had burned so fiercely she was exhausted. Her shoulders slumped. "There were no names mentioned in it except for Lieutenant O'Neil's. And there was a phone number to call if you thought you could help the police." She licked her dry lips. "I called it."

Mike stiffened. Whenever he was backed into a corner and saw no way out, all his well-practiced defenses snapped into place. He was at his strongest under pressure. The worse the situation the better he functioned, and this time was no exception.

"So, the police told you to forget it and you came here to confront me instead?"

"I just came for your help."

"Oh." The smile on Mike's lips was so stiff, so uncharacteristic of the gentleness she loved about him, Amy was put off. She stared, unable to reconcile the tender man she knew with the hardened individual she was facing. For the first time since she'd noticed it, the scar on Mike's face seemed to fit his image.

She tried once more. "Please?"

"Go home, Amy. You've gotten yourself all worked up over nothing. Go home and forget it."

Coming from a stranger, from someone other than Mike, the advice might have been easier to take. The trouble was, the more Amy concentrated on what he'd told her, on the way he was acting, the more confused she became.

Mike went to the door, opened it for her and waited while she slowly crossed the room. Hold on, he told himself. You can make it. You can't let her see any weakness, any vacilation. Not when she's so close to buying your story.

Amy lifted her eyes to him as she passed. They were moist with tears and so full of sorrow Mike thought his own heart would burst.

Before he realized what he was doing he'd laid his hand on her upper arm and he searched his mind for some casual remark to accompany the touch. "Say hello to Seymour for me, will you?"

"Later." Amy heard the somber tone of her voice and accepted it as being preferable to anger. "I have to go to work now."

"Good. I have a meeting with a client at seven tonight. Maybe we'll drop in to Marino's for dinner."

Irony seized her. For weeks she'd watched the restaurant door for Mike to appear and spent the rest of the time listening for her phone to ring, hoping he'd return. Now he really was the *last* person she wanted to see.

"I wish you wouldn't," Amy said flatly. "The steaks at the Pines are every bit as good. Go there instead."

"All right." Nodding, he walked with her to the outer door and continued to watch after her as she disappeared down the street and around the corner. She never once looked back.

In silent rage, Mike drove his fist hard against the doorjamb, an avalanche of curses swirling through his mind. Nice work, Dixon, he told himself. Real neat. There was obviously another clipping, and you missed it. You may not be through paying for your carelessness.

How could he convince Amy that what he was doing was for her own good without letting her know too much?

"Simple," he answered, clenching his jaw and going inside. He couldn't.

Chapter Seven

For Amy, the walk from Mike's office to Marino's was interminable. Why had he lied to her? Worse, why had he refused to divulge the truth when she'd confronted him with the news of her conversation with Finch? Mike was supposed to be her friend and she his. What had gone wrong?

Amy sighed and increased her pace. Agonizing over the apparent mistake her heart had made in trusting Mike Dixon was getting her nowhere. She couldn't change her lingering feelings of betrayal any more than she could go back in time and change the facts of her birth—whatever they were.

Picturing Mike's face in the final moments before she'd turned away, Amy recalled traces of emotional involvement she'd been too overwrought to notice then. Oh, the hardness had remained, Mike's armor was securely in place, yet in his eyes there had been a glimmer of something else. Something not tender as much as it was soberly perceptive.

She straight-armed her way through the heavy mahogany door and found Marissa ensconced behind the counter in Marino's entry hall. It took a few seconds for Amy's eyes to adjust to the dim light inside the restaurant.

"Well?" Marissa's expression was expectant.

Amy joined her, tossed her purse beneath the counter and slid shut the security door on the cabinet. "Well, what?"

"You come bursting in here like the wild Santa Ana winds off the desert and you ask me, well, what?" She took Amy's arm. "Come on. Give. Where were you?"

"Search International."

"Need I ask with who?"

"Whom." Amy was trying to be pleasant, but her mood refused to cooperate.

"Whatever," Marissa said, undaunted. She cocked her head, staring. "I'd guess, from the look on your face, that your meeting didn't go all that well."

"You'd be right." Amy took a deep, settling breath. It didn't help quiet her conscience one bit. "I think I just lost a friend, Marissa, but I couldn't help it. Sometimes he makes me so *mad*."

"You've still got me."

Amy tried to force a chuckle. "No offense, but it's not the same."

The younger woman rolled her eyes. "I know. If I had a shot at a guy like Mike Dixon I'd do whatever it took to make the relationship work, believe me."

"Even if you were sure he'd lied to you?" Leaning against the counter, Amy steadied herself. The trauma of her encounter with Mike was just beginning to break through the cushion of adrenaline that had kept her going, and she felt a bit unsteady.

"Maybe," Marissa said. "I suppose it would depend on how important the lie was to me." She paused, her hand tightening on Amy's arm. "He's not married, is he?"

"It was nothing like that." Retrieving her purse, Amy withdrew the clipping and gave it to Marissa. "I found this in my father's papers."

Marissa scanned it quickly. "So?"

"So, I think I may be one of those babies and I think Mike knows it."

Silent, Marissa scowled at Amy.

"Well, say something," Amy demanded. "Tell me I'm nuts or agree with me that Mike is probably lying, but don't just stand there!"

Marissa shook her head. "Nope. You're the one who has to decide who and what is important to you. I wouldn't dream of trying to influence you one way or the other. If you don't love Mike, then . . ."

"Whoa! Wait just a minute. Who said I loved him?"

"In words—no one. But who was it who stormed in here, fuming, then practically fell apart when she tried to tell me the man was history?"

Smiling, she gave Amy's arm a pat. "Tell you what, as soon as you decide what's most important to you—Mike or some imagined sin he may or may not have committed—you let me know and we'll finish this discussion."

"You'd have to have been there," Amy insisted. "He was so unreasonably unbending I hardly recognized him."

"He's a *man*," Marissa explained as if to a child. "They don't react the same way we women do. You can't always look at them and figure out what they're thinking or feeling." She chuckled. "Heck . . . *most* of the time you can't. Don't expect Mike to make sense to you, Amy. Just accept him as he is and get on with your life."

"Even if he doesn't trust me enough to level with me?"

Marissa vigorously nodded. "Yeah. Why not? What have you got to lose?"

"Just my heart, I guess," Amy said wryly. "And you and I both know it's too late to prevent the loss of that, don't we?"

Sniffling once, she stared at the clipping in disgust then stuffed it into her purse, exchanging it for a tissue.

"Hey," Marissa said lightly. "Knock off the crying."

"I'm not crying." She made a silly face and blew her nose. "I have allergies."

"To spring flower pollens?"

Amy snickered. "No." She pitched the tissue into the trash. "To the thought of giving up on Mike Dixon."

The week at Marino's had been busy, as usual, but no amount of hectic activity was enough to pry Amy's mind from thoughts of Mike for very long. Every man who remotely resembled him made her heart skip beats, and every male voice deeper than a boy's gave her the shivers.

It had just happened again, causing her to mumble expletives she *never* used and call herself every kind of a fool. She turned to Marissa. "Do you know I still haven't heard a word from that stinker."

"Mike?"

Amy threw her friend a melodramatic, comical pout. "How did you know?"

"It was a lucky guess," Marissa said. "Anyway, I wouldn't worry. He'll call."

Tossing her head, Amy rolled her eyes with an exaggerated flourish. "I wish I believed that."

"So, give in and make the first move."

"After the awful way I acted?" Chagrin filled Amy's expression. "I honestly can't remember half of what I said to the poor man, but I'm certain it was dreadful."

The younger woman shrugged. "I'll bet he's heard worse in his line of work." She giggled. "*Much* worse."

"Probably," Amy agreed. "I sent him to the Pines, you know."

Marissa gasped. "The competition! Oh, Amy, that *is* bad."

"All right, all right. Don't be sarcastic. Besides, the steaks are good over there. So's the prime rib."

"Alonzo would murder you for a comment like that," Marissa observed. "You'd better watch out."

"Yeah." She chuckled. "And if I'm about to be murdered, I really should make peace with my enemies, shouldn't I?"

"I wouldn't exactly call Mike your enemy."

Amy gave her a friendly poke on the arm. "How did you get so smart?"

"Life," Marissa said. "I have a funny feeling I've lived a bit more than you have, even if I am younger."

"Is it that obvious?" Coloring, Amy began to fuss with the toothpick dispenser and business card display on the counter.

"Well..." Kindly, Marissa touched Amy's shoulder. "I'd be glad to listen if you'd like to talk some more. You know, the intimate stuff."

Amy's laugh was nervous. "There isn't any intimate stuff. Not really." She felt her cheeks growing hot and she peered from side to side to make sure no one was close enough to overhear. "If I tell you something private, do you promise to keep my secret?"

"Cross my heart and hope to die."

Hesitating only a moment, Amy licked her lips and began. "Okay, here goes. I was pretty young when my father had his stroke, and between finishing school and caring for him, I just never...I mean, there was no opportunity to get close to a man, at least not in a physical way, so I never..."

Marissa's hands flattened over her heart and she gasped. "Oh, my God! You're a *virgin*!"

Amy grabbed her. "Shush! Quiet! Do you think I want the whole world to know?"

"More importantly, does Mike know?" Marissa asked.

"Would it matter?"

"It might. At least to an honorable man."

"He's guessed," Amy said softly.

"And just when did this interesting subject come up?" Leaning forward on the glass counter, Marissa listened intently.

"When we were kissing."

"Kissing, or..."

"Just kissing, okay?" Amy took a few steps away from her friend, then turned with a silly grin spreading across her face. "Darn it."

"Oh, boy." Marissa was smiling broadly. "Your life is getting more interesting than the soaps I watch on my days off."

"Thanks," she said wryly. "What do you think one of those women would do in my place?"

"Never mind them. What do *you* want to do?"

"I want to call and apologize to Mike. But what if he hangs up on me?"

"And if you don't call him, if you never hear from him again? What then?"

"You have a point there," Amy admitted. She stepped out from behind the counter. "Watch the front for me?"

"While you make a phone call?" Marissa's grin threatened to split her rosy cheeks.

Amy nodded. She was already halfway across the entry hall on her way to the privacy of her office. "While I try to fix one of the worst mistakes of my entire life."

Mike's voice was polite when he took Amy's call, and although he seemed as unsure as she was of how to proceed, Amy was certain she detected traces of emotion he couldn't conceal.

"I'm glad you agreed to talk to me," she said. "I was a little afraid you wouldn't."

"Nonsense." He sat back, cradling the receiver and picturing her lovely face. "You know I'll always be there for you, Amy."

"Always is a long time," she said quietly. "What I had in mind is more current." His silence spurred her on. "The telephone is fine for some things but I'd rather be face to face when I apologize for my behavior the other day. If you're free tomorrow evening, I'd like to fix dinner for you."

"That's not necessary," Mike said. "Neither is an apology."

"I suppose not, but I really would like to see you."

"Not because you feel an obligation?" he asked.

"Not entirely. I mean, that was why I called you in the first place but I do enjoy your company."

"You don't have to do this, Amy. I'm not angry with you. Your reactions were perfectly normal."

"Not for me, they weren't," she explained. "I don't make a habit of accusing my friends of treachery."

But that was exactly the crime of which he was guilty, Mike reminded himself. He had purposely deceived her. And his guilt for doing it refused to go away. The nicer Amy was to him, the more forgiving, the worse he ultimately felt about the way he'd treated her.

"Are you sure you want me to come to your house for dinner?" he asked. "We could go out."

She shook her head. "No. Please. I have some things to say to you that are best said in private."

Private. Mike's pulse raced. The last thing he needed was another private encounter with the one woman who made him doubt the wisdom of relying solely on himself, the one person in whose presence he was beginning to feel safe about revealing his innermost thoughts.

"Is that wise, Amy?" Her soft laughter sent a chill up his spine.

"Probably not, but since when have I acted smart where you're concerned? Anyway, Seymour is practically a teenager now, and he misses you terribly."

"*He* misses me?"

"Uh-huh. He's not sleeping well and he paces the floor a lot, mumbling your name."

"I see. Then I guess I'd better agree to come," Mike said. "For his sake."

"Absolutely," Amy replied. "He'll be thrilled."

"And will you?" Mike's voice was husky, low, vibrant with remembered desire.

"Yes," she confessed easily. "I already am."

Not wanting to appear too formal, Mike had decided to wear a turtleneck under his sport jacket. That way, he reasoned, if he and Amy ultimately decided to go dancing or something, he'd still be adequately dressed.

Fidgety, he recombed his hair, stared at his image in his car's rearview mirror and cursed.

"Damn it. You can't continue to put her off," he told himself. "Amy deserves the truth. She's earned it, and Ray Alexander owes it to her."

Mike climbed out of the car in front of Amy's duplex and slammed the door. For twenty-three years she'd been lied to, and it was high time she was privy to the facts concerning the man she'd come to know as her father.

Little doubt remained as to what Ray had done, and Mike's simmering anger surfaced. "Criminal" was too mild a description for it. A man who trafficked in innocent human lives deserved no one's loyalty, least of all his.

As Mike walked past the palms and cacti artistically scattered amid the rocks in Amy's yard and started to climb the stairs, the front door opened. His first vision of Amy made him forget everything else.

She was wearing a lacy, cream-colored dress that fit so well it looked like it had been made just for her. Dropping off her shoulders, the dress clung to her waist, then flared into a flowingly feminine skirt. High-heeled white sandals made her legs appear longer, more graceful than ever.

His eyes traveled up to link with hers. There was a look of happy expectation on her face.

Neither of them moved, and Amy wondered if the entire earth had ceased its revolutions, so suspended was her entire universe. It would be easy to throw herself into Mike's embrace, yet she feared his rejection. Better to stand and wonder than to make the wrong move and banish all doubt.

Mike saw her start toward him then change her mind before her feet had taken a full step. Being apart was agony for both of them, and he couldn't resist opening his arms to her. "Come here."

In an instant, Amy crossed the void between them and flew into his embrace, clinging to him unashamedly. Her cheek was pressed to his chest when she said, "Oh, Mike. I'm so sorry."

"So am I, honey," he replied, burying his face in her flowing hair to kiss her neck. "So am I."

"I missed you." She snuggled closer.

"Me, too." Mike released her reluctantly. "Would you like to go dancing after dinner?" He cocked one eyebrow as he looked her up and down. "That's some dress."

Amy chuckled. "I hoped you'd like it. I know I shouldn't admit this, but I bought it to impress you."

"You got your money's worth," Mike said. "I'm impressed."

"Good. I hope my cooking will do as well."

With his arm at her waist, Mike followed her into the house. "No chance. That dress wins no matter what's for dinner."

"Terrific," Amy shot back. "I slave over a hot stove all day and you refuse to be overwhelmed. Fine thing."

Mike took a deep breath, enjoying the aromas of home cooking as he looked around the now familiar living room. Overwhelmed was exactly how he'd felt the first time Amy's home had triggered his childhood memories.

Now, he was no less cognizant of the nostalgic feelings that pulled at him. He simply accepted them. Everything about Amy Alexander made him feel wanted. When he was with her it was as if he'd finally come home after an eternity of being away.

She'd started for the kitchen. Mike pursued her and brought her back. Holding both her hands, he said, "Wait. I owe you an explanation."

"It's not necessary." She smiled benevolently. "I was wrong to suspect you of lying to me."

"No. No, you weren't." He carefully watched her face. She seemed ready to accept whatever he told her, so Mike forged ahead.

"You see, I *did* go to see Finch about your case."

"Mine? But that means . . ."

He quieted her with the briefest of kisses. "Hush. Let me finish."

Amy nodded.

"Remember that big sheet of newspaper you had? Well, I read it and then burned it."

Her eyes widened, questioning without words.

"The paper mentioned a rash of kidnappings, some of them from the nursery at Mercy Hospital, and the clue of finding it among your father's possessions was just too strong to pass up."

"Oh, Mike." Her vision misted. "You're not saying that I really was one of those babies, are you?"

He hedged, frowning. "I thought it might be a possibility."

Amy could no longer contain the tears that slid silently down her cheeks.

"Hey, don't," Mike said lightly. "You'll ruin your pretty dress."

"Do you think I care about a dress now?" she sobbed.

No. He didn't think that of her. A person as naturally loving as Amy would always consider other people's feelings before material possessions. He should have realized that earlier and spared her.

He was thankful that there was still time to stop and rescue the situation. To continue would be to destroy the memory of the two people most precious to Amy—her adoptive parents. Mike couldn't do that to her. The truth mattered far less than Amy's ultimate happiness—*or* his own.

Mike's thumbs caught her tears and wiped them away. "There's no need for that," he soothed. "You didn't let me finish. I looked into the case thoroughly and found out it was nothing but a silly coincidence. Really."

She sniffled, staring into his eyes and finding the honesty she yearned to see. "You're sure?"

"Positive. Your parents must have been curious about the missing babies, that's all. Anyway, there was absolutely no evidence tying them to the disappearances." Except that the law firm your father worked for was suspected of being a front for black-market baby sales, he added silently.

"Why didn't you say so in the first place?" Amy asked, drawing the back of her hand across her cheek to dry her tears.

Mike thought fast. "I didn't want to upset you until I was sure, and I certainly didn't want you to think I was trying to discredit your father." The thankful look on Amy's face nearly melted his heart.

"Oh, Mike. You're so sweet to care about him like that." She reached up to brush a kiss across Mike's cheek. "Dad really was special, you know. I couldn't have asked for a better father—or mother."

"I'm sure you couldn't," he said, retreating from her, searching for a suitable distraction. "And now that we've settled all that, where's dinner? I'm starved."

Taking his hand, Amy led him into the kitchen. Rousing himself from his bed in the corner by the stove, Seymour arched his back, stretched and eyed Mike cautiously.

"I don't think he remembers me," Mike observed. "Has it been that long since I visited him?"

"Sixteen days," she said, checking her wristwatch, "four hours and twenty-two minutes."

"Too long, huh?" he asked.

With Mike beside her again, Amy felt so wonderful she was surprised that her feet were still touching the ground.

She smiled at him. "Much too long."

Mike stiffened, hoping Amy didn't notice his tenseness. He had missed her terribly, yet he'd purposely let the days and hours pass, hoping the urge to return to her would eventually pass. It hadn't.

When she'd telephoned he'd reacted to the sound of her voice the way he sometimes did to the voices in his dreams, voices from the distant past. Being with Amy was making him remember, making him see his loneliness, and he wasn't sure he liked the questions he'd been asking himself lately.

Her touch on his arm was light. Startled, Mike jumped.

"I'm sorry," Amy said. "You suddenly seemed so sad I was worried." Encouraged when Mike laid his hand over hers she asked, "You were miles away just now, weren't you?"

"I guess I was."

This was as close as Amy had ever felt to Mike. She was basking in the intimacy when a terrible thought occurred to her. Maybe Mike had been hesitant to let her into his life because he did already have a wife or a lover! She knew Marissa would have plunged ahead without asking, but Amy Alexander had to know.

"Is it because there's someone else in your life? I mean, I'm not trying to intrude, but . . ." The words trailed off to a whisper. Oh, God, she prayed, let me be wrong. Let him be unattached.

Mike snorted and patted her hand. "No, honey. You're probably not going to believe this, but I was thinking about my mother."

Relief flooded through Amy, body and soul. "Oh, Mike. She must be a wonderful woman to have produced a son like you. Tell me about her."

He shook his head and turned away. "There's nothing to tell. She died when I was six years old."

He opened the refrigerator door. "So, what'll it be?" he asked with false cheerfulness. "Are we having coffee with dinner, or shall I open this handy bottle of Chablis?"

Chapter Eight

Mike was so upbeat and jovial throughout dinner Amy felt as if she were dining stageside at a comedy club. There was no doubt he was trying to convince her he was enjoying himself. But Amy knew he wasn't.

The dining room was lighted by a chandelier, and she'd also placed lighted candles in the center of the round table. Her best linen cloth was crowded with platters and bowls of food enough for four people. She hadn't been certain how much Mike might eat and she wasn't about to be caught short. She shook her head as she blotted her lips with a napkin. His appetite seemed good enough. It was his mood that was strange.

Amy offered him more of the main course. She'd fixed fried chicken because it was the one dish in her culinary repertoire she was positive would be delicious. It had been her father's favorite, and the echo of his generous compliments had filled her memory as she'd lovingly prepared the meal.

Mike waved off another helping. "Thanks, but I'm stuffed. It was delicious!" he exclaimed for what had to be the seventh or eighth time. Leaning back, he placed his napkin beside his empty plate. "You're a great cook, Amy."

"I'm glad you liked it." She stood, reached for two of the serving dishes and smiled at him. "I've been thinking—"

"Uh-oh. *Now* we're in trouble," he quipped, his voice strained and overly loud.

"Hush," Amy ordered. "I'm trying to be serious for a minute."

That's what I was afraid of, Mike thought, taking care to keep his smile securely in place. He expanded his grin and held up his hands in surrender. "Okay. Shoot."

"Is your offer to take me dancing still good?"

Relief flowed through Mike. Dancing! Dear Lord, he was finally going to be able to gracefully escape Amy's house and the ghosts of his past!

"Sure," he answered quickly. "If you want to go dancing, we'll go."

Her brow creased. "I thought *you* wanted to go."

"I do. I do." Mike was on his feet, stacking dirty dishes. "We'll be off as soon as I help you clean up this mess."

Moving rapidly he made two trips to Amy's one, arranging most of the glasses and dishes in her dishwasher. "There. Ready to go?"

"As soon as I freshen my lipstick." She handed him what was left of the fruit salad they'd eaten for dessert. "Here. Stick this in the refrigerator."

"Sure. Be glad to," he said, complying. Amy left the room.

As soon as he was alone, Mike felt his shoulders slump and he let the breath out of his lungs in an audible moan. This was it. The end. Tonight was positively the last time he was going to allow himself the luxury of seeing Amy Alexander. The experience was too hard on him.

Mike stared out the window. The next thing he knew, Amy would be asking about the rest of his life, about his childhood . . . about his father.

His fingers found and traced the scar on his cheek. His father. What a joke.

When he heard the tap of Amy's heels on the floor behind him he steeled himself against her charms, against the gentleness in her that had led him to speak about the death of his mother for the first time in years. He didn't need pity, Amy's or anyone's. Attachments to family might be fine for other people but they had no place in *his* life.

Careful to display a broad smile, Mike turned. "Ready?" Amy had wrapped a fringed magenta shawl around her shoulders, drawing it close by tying it in the front. The bright color made her skin glow, her eyes sparkle more radiantly than ever.

Perhaps it was the knowledge that after tonight he'd never have the chance to hold her in his arms again that made Mike's gut tie in a hard knot. Or maybe it was simply the image of Amy surrounded by a home filled with love. He didn't know. He only knew that once again he wanted what he could never hope to possess.

For a few seconds after Mike turned to look at her, Amy stared. So much raw emotion was reflected in his eyes she questioned vaguely if he'd actually wept while they were apart. Suddenly, the anguish and torment were so effectively wiped away she wondered if she'd imagined them. In their place was a masterful, commanding aura that betrayed none of the turmoil she'd glimpsed.

"I'm ready if you are," she said.

"Definitely." Mike took her arm and led her quickly to the front door. "Don't wait up for us, Seymour," he called. "We're going to dance all night."

Pausing before slamming the door behind them, he asked, "Got your key?"

Amy nodded and patted the evening bag she carried. "Be sure the door latches. It's old and tricky sometimes." She spotted Mrs. Norton peeking from her side of the house and waved a cheery goodbye.

Saluting the elderly busybody, Mike cupped his hand around his mouth to shout, "Don't *you* wait up, either. We'll be late."

"You're crazy," Amy said, laughing and dragging him down the steps.

"Why? We don't want her to worry, do we?"

"I doubt she worries," Amy countered. "I lead a pretty sedate life—most of the time."

"Sedate?" He eyed the Jaguar parked in the driveway. "Not from where I stand, you don't."

"Shall we take my car? You can drive it if you'd like."

"Would I!"

Settling himself behind the wheel Mike forgot to open the passenger door for Amy. Not one to stand on ceremony, she laughed and let herself in. "Don't forget me." She jingled her key ring. "I have the keys."

"Oops. Sorry." Mike's hands were caressing the leather-clad steering wheel. "Now that I've demonstrated my total lack of manners, where shall we go?"

Amy laughed again. "I hate to suggest it, but the Pines has a dance floor and a decent band."

"How would you know that?"

"I have my spies."

Starting the car, Mike gunned the motor before he backed down the driveway. Once into traffic he was cautious but aggressive, handling the Jaguar expertly.

"Uh-oh. Have I created a monster?"

"You may have," Mike admitted. "I've lied to myself about what I really wanted every time I've bought a new car."

"Then maybe it's time you freed yourself to have what you want," Amy said quietly.

Remaining silent, Mike made a tight turn onto Tahquitz-McCallum Way, downshifted and pressed the accelerator to the floor. The engine roared, carrying them faster and faster up the canyon road away from town.

He's *running*, Amy decided, suddenly seeing possible reasons for Mike's behavior more clearly, and he has been ever since you've known him! Manipulating the power of the car's engine is only the outward sign of the battle he's waging with himself.

She chanced a sidelong glance. Mike's jaw was set, his hands firm on the wheel. If only he'd let her through his defenses, she was certain he'd find comfort in sharing whatever was bothering him. And she'd know, too, how best to help him.

Frustrated, Amy leaned back in the seat to watch the road. Mike had come a step closer to accepting her when he'd mentioned the loss of his mother. Yet that very act of admission had rebounded to make him pretend a joviality he didn't feel and make him far less the amiable companion he was trying to be.

Marissa would tell me I'm nuts, Amy mused. Accept him, she'd say. Don't worry, she'd say.

Amy clasped her hands in her lap. Until she'd begun to love Mike, she'd easily been able to take him at face value and not fret over his happiness. Now everything was different. When he hurt, *she* hurt. It was that simple. And right now, Mike Dixon was hurting plenty.

The Pines would have been an apt name if the vegetation planted around the restaurant had been more suited to the desert climate. As it was, the few surviving trees were scraggly, twisted junipers.

Romantically rustic, with a peaked roof and rough-hewn wooden siding, the restaurant lay in a hollow, surrounded by hills dotted with boulders and cacti. Even in the heat of the day the sprawling building garnered some shade and

Amy had often wished she could pick up Marino's and plunk it down in as inspiring a place as this.

Grinning sheepishly, Mike remembered to open the passenger door this time. "Better?"

"I didn't mind your momentary lapse," Amy said. "I'm glad you enjoyed the drive."

"I didn't scare you?"

It's not your driving that scares me, she thought, but kept her conclusions to herself. "No."

"Then let's go inside. The desert is chilly once the sun goes down."

"That's one of the things I like about it," Amy said, preceding him down the stone path from the parking lot. She felt a flutter of nervousness before she added, "What originally brought you to Palm Springs?"

"Money." Mike laughed quietly.

"Not everyone in this town is loaded, you know. What about all the support people in the stores and service industry?"

Ushering her inside the restaurant, he bent low to whisper in her ear. "Don't tell anyone, but I have a sliding scale. Not all my clients pay the same rates."

She wasn't at all surprised by Mike's fairness and sensitivity. "Then I must be at the very bottom," Amy said. "Because you haven't charged me a thing."

Mike held up two fingers to the hostess, and they were led to a small, round table next to the dance floor while he continued his conversation with Amy. "I told you. I don't work for you."

"Would you, if I asked?" She seated herself in the chair he held out for her then watched his expression as he joined her.

Mike cocked his head toward the polished wooden floor beside their table. The trio on the raised bandstand in the corner was playing a slow, melodic air featuring a smiling musician on the keyboard. An older, leathery-faced guitar player and a middle-aged black man on drums provided backup. One other couple was already dancing.

"I would *dance*, if you asked," he said. "Shall we?"

"All right." Amy untied her shawl and left it on the chair. Myriad questions were tumbling through her mind, questions Mike was far too adept at sidestepping. Under the present circumstances she saw little point in asking any of them. When he was ready, he'd tell her all she wanted to know. Until then, it would have to be enough just to be near him.

She stepped into the circle of his arms and closed her eyes, letting him guide her movements, and heard his sharp intake of breath. Their bodies fit together the way she had remembered—no, *better* than that. It was as if they were one.

This time, she carefully made no move to respond beyond the natural swaying of her body in time with the music. She wasn't going to give him any excuse to pull away. If he wanted a kiss he'd have to take it, then the responsibility would be strictly his.

It wasn't long before Amy was regretting her decision. Together, she and Mike were so perfect, each so attuned to every nuance, every breath of the other, that it seemed as if their hearts had even begun to beat with the same cadence.

When he placed her hand on his chest, released it there and wrapped both his arms around her to draw her closer, she wondered how much more her senses could take before the sweet torment drove her insane.

Amy spread her fingers, her palms resting on the warmth radiating through Mike's knit shirt, and she found herself wishing it had buttons down the front instead of being a turtleneck so she could slip her fingers inside and better caress him.

Unconsciously, she moved her hands over the expanse of his chest and rested her forehead in the hollow of his shoulder. The band was playing a slow song, but her breathing had grown rapid. In her mind she could picture the muscular torso she knew he possessed. In her heart, she had already given herself to him.

Mike's body was taut with desire, his mind focused on only Amy. It was a damned good thing they were in a public place, he told himself, or he'd be in big trouble.

Nonsense, his logical side tried to argue. She's just a woman, no different than any other woman.

Mike felt himself draw a ragged breath. No. Amy *was* different, and it was that difference that would keep him from her bed ... from her life.

But it's not over yet, he added. We have tonight. Now. And being with her was the most agonizingly exquisite experience of his life.

He held her through dance after dance until he'd lost count of the number. Finally, wiping perspiration from their brows and loosening their neckties, the band took a break.

"I was hoping they'd play all night," Amy said dreamily. Preceding Mike to their table, she noticed for the first time the baskets of live plants hanging from the rafters and the subtle suggestions of outdoors in the open beams and planks on the walls.

"Maybe if I tip them enough, they will." Mike seated her first, then circled the table to face her. He wanted to drink in the sight of her until he was intoxicated with it. After all, the lovely, mind's-eye view had to last him a lifetime.

A waiter appeared, and Mike deferred to Amy. "Wine?"

"No, I don't think that's a good idea," she said with a demure smile. "I already feel a little tipsy."

"Must be the Chablis we had with dinner," he said, ordering iced tea for both of them. "I feel it, too."

"Do you?" Her eyes lifted to meet his, pleading for a word from him, a sign that he understood that what they were feeling had nothing to do with alcohol.

Mike's voice was low, his gaze so intense Amy felt its potent pervasiveness in every nerve.

"Yes," he said, "but it will pass. You know it will."

Positive they had long ago stopped discussing wine, she tried to smile. "I don't want those feelings to go away."

"We can't always have what we want." Somber, Mike took her hands, enfolding them.

Lacing his fingers through hers, he sent her a look of such disturbing intensity that it reached into her core and fanned the smoldering embers of desire there until she wanted to throw herself into his arms and cling forever.

"We can try," she whispered. "Can't we?"

"It won't work, Amy," he said, shaking his head as he tenderly caressed her hands. "Some dreams are best left unspoiled and unfulfilled."

"Then what's the point of dreaming?" she asked.

Arching one eyebrow, Mike brought her hands to his lips and brushed a kiss across her knuckles. "There is no point," he said slowly. "Dreams are for children."

"In that case, I don't ever want to grow up."

Mike released her and sat back in his chair. "Maybe that kind of reasoning works for you, Amy. I learned a long time ago it doesn't work for me."

When the band resumed playing, Mike stood and wordlessly held out his hand to Amy. Grasping it tightly she let him lead her to the dance floor and stepped, once again, into the shelter of his arms.

Most of the music was slow, romantic, and she was engulfed by the blissful rapture of Mike's presence. They sat out the more upbeat songs by mutual consent.

The waiter had cleared away the remnants of the New York-style cheesecake they'd eaten as a midnight snack and refilled their glasses more times than Amy could count. She barely noticed when he approached their table again.

"I'm sorry sir, madam, but we're closing in fifteen minutes. Can I get you anything else?"

Mike caught Amy's negative shake of the head and answered for both of them. "No, thank you. We'll be leaving after one last dance."

This time, Amy was ahead of him when they stepped onto the polished wooden floor. She turned, reaching to wind her arms around Mike's neck, and thought for a moment he might kiss her.

He didn't. Coming to her in two rapid strides, he enclosed her in a tight embrace, bending to lay his head beside hers, and pressed his lips into the hollow of her shoulder.

Amy's eyes closed. Love surrounded her—it was unmistakable and so strong it was almost palpable. The way he was holding her, the way his warm breath rushed against her skin, the way his pounding heart pressed against her breasts, crushing them, she knew. No matter what he said or did, Mike Dixon loved her as much as she loved him. Oh, maybe he showed it differently, maybe he always would, but that didn't make it any less real.

"Mike?" she whispered. Snuggling her lips close to his ear, Amy teased him with her mouth.

"Um?"

"I want you to know something." It was time he faced their feelings, Amy reasoned. Time she made him see that lovely dreams could be his, too, if only he would open his heart and mind to their possibilities. Time he confessed how much he loved her.

"Sh." He pressed his face closer, not daring to look into her eyes, not daring to let her speak. "Don't talk, please, Amy."

"Oh, Mike, why won't you let me get close to you?" she pleaded.

His arms tightened around her body in a crush that left her breathless. "We're close, honey. Real close. Can't you tell?" With a smile he straightened. "Any closer, and you'd be dancing *behind* me!"

"Stop joking!" Would he *never* take her seriously? Amy pushed on his chest and was surprised when he relinquished his hold on her without argument.

"What's the matter?"

"Nothing," she said quietly. She was embarrassed by her eruption of anger but accepted her feelings as natural. She had to stand up to him or lose her self-respect.

Stalking to the table she swung her shawl around her shoulders. "Take me home, Mike."

"Sure." He tossed some folded bills on the table and followed her to the door. "We've closed the place, anyway."

By the time they'd reached her house on Calle El Segundo, Amy was penitent. She wasn't going to reach Mike at all if she didn't control her frustration. He wasn't like other people. He couldn't be expected to react predictably. Yet it was his difference that had made him so understanding, so empathetic about other people's problems. There was a tender side to Mike that he couldn't hide no matter how hard he tried. Amy intended to appeal to that part of him. *If* he'd listen.

Stopping the car in her driveway, he kept the keys as he ushered her to her door.

"Which one?" Mike asked, holding the key ring up in the faint glow from the porch light.

"The brass one," she said. "Next to the little one."

"Got it." He bent and unlocked the door, then tried to pass the ring to Amy with no success.

She bolted through the door, leaving it standing open behind her and Mike hesitating alone on the porch. "Just toss them on the bench in the entry," she called back. "How do you take your coffee? Black?"

"I can't stay."

"Nonsense. I'm wide awake, and so are you. I'll make us some coffee, and we can sit and talk."

"No, Amy."

Peeking aorund the corner from the kitchen she flashed him her brightest smile. "No, what? No coffee?"

"No conversation," he said. "I have to be going."

She laughed at his stiff posture. "Don't be so tense. Loosen up. I won't bite."

"I'm not so sure of that." Mike felt something lean against the bottom of his pant leg. Seymour was yawning and rubbing by him, so Mike picked him up before he entered the kitchen.

"We woke the poor baby," he said, lowering the cat to the kitchen floor and gently releasing him with a pat on the head.

"Then we're even," Amy told Mike. "He's in the habit of jumping on my bed in the middle of the night and wanting to play."

"I can understand that." Mike began to relax. If Amy had decided to lighten up from her serious mood at the Pines, he had no objection to spending a little more time with her.

He wasn't ready to admit how hard it was to face walking out on her forever. He refused to think of their situation with finality. He'd just spend a few more minutes with Amy, bid her a pleasant good night, and that would be that. She'd get over him soon enough.

"Why?" Amy asked, giggling. "Do you like to jump on sleeping women?"

"Not on a regular basis," Mike said with a half smile. "It's usually preferable if they're awake."

"I see." She paused. Careful. He's in a better mood, now. Don't spoil it. Keep it casual and silly or you'll lose him again. "And is there someone you jump on regularly?"

"Why?"

"No reason. I just thought, if there was, I'd see if I couldn't convince her to move to Siberia or something."

"Nice place, Siberia. Good skiing."

"So I've heard." Amy watched Mike for a change of expression and saw none. "So, shall I buy her a ticket?"

Snorting, Mike shook his head. "Naw. Save your money. The only woman in my life is Marie, my secretary, and she's happily married with six grown children."

The only woman in my life, he'd said. So what was *she*, chopped liver? as Marissa would ask so colorfully. Too bad she couldn't phone Marissa for advice about how to behave, Amy thought. It was hard to rely on your own instincts when they'd failed you so often in the past, at least where Mike Dixon was concerned.

"Six children, huh? Must be nice to be part of a family like that. I always wanted a brother or sister." She smiled at Seymour who was stalking an imaginary quarry through the doorway into the darkened living room. "As you know, my parents never even offered me a puppy!"

"I had a buddy in the Army who told me he'd figured out a way around that when he was a kid," Mike said with a wry smile. "He said he wanted a dog, so he badgered his folks unmercifully for a baby brother and they bought him a puppy to make him forget about wanting a human playmate."

Amy clasped her hands together in delight. "You're kidding! What a wonderful idea."

"Remember that if someday your own children try the same trick."

She turned then to get coffee mugs out of the cupboard, speaking with her back to Mike to insure that her tone of voice remained casual. "I think I would like to have at least two children. Being raised alone has its drawbacks."

"You can't blame anything on the other kid."

"Were you an only child, too?" Amy turned, still purposely avoiding eye contact with Mike.

"Yes."

She poured hot coffee into both mugs. "It's tough, huh? I wish my parents had seen fit to adopt a second time. They always told me they couldn't have another child because they were too old." Amy turned, handing one steaming mug to Mike then curling her fingers around the other.

"Oh, I don't know," Mike observed, staring into the steam wafting from his cup. "You probably matured faster being the only child among adults. I've read that firstborns and single children in families are the greatest achievers."

"You mean, maybe I have the managerial position at Marino's because I had no siblings?"

"It could be."

Sighing, Amy led the way to the small pedestal table in the corner of her kitchen and seated herself, gesturing to Mike to follow. "Of course, it's also possible that I'm the product of the genetic traits inherited from my birth parents."

He joined her, resting his elbows on the table. "Probably both."

"I should press the search for them, you know," Amy said absently. "They might care what's happened to me."

"And, face it, they might not," Mike said soberly.

"But don't you think all parents care some?" She raised her inquiring gaze to his. "I mean, I am their daughter."

Mike's jaw tightened, and so did his grip on the mug. "No. I don't. There are all kinds of parents in the world, Amy. *Lots* of them don't give a damn about the children they've produced."

She reached across to him. "You can't mean that. I know you're bitter because your mother died so young, but what about your father? Surely he—"

"Drop it," Mike ordered. He stood. "I should have known better than to come in for coffee and conversation." He stressed the last word. "You just can't leave it alone, can you?"

"Please, Mike." Amy stretched out her hand to him, but he backed away.

"Please, what? Please tell you all about my life? And then what would you do? Pity me? Save me from myself? No,

thanks, Ms Alexander. I don't need saving. I'm doing just
fine as I am.''

"I never said you weren't.''

Amy watched as Mike spun on his heel and strode rapidly away. More angry at herself for asking than she was at
Mike for his irate response, Amy felt suddenly weak and had
to lean on the table to keep her balance. Maybe she had been
wrong to quiz Mike about his past, yet how could she expect
to relate to him in the future if she always had to be so careful about what she did or didn't say?

What future? her heart countered. He just stormed out of
here, totally disgusted with you for prying. What makes you
think he's not gone for good?

Tears gathered in Amy's eyes while she tried to imagine
Mike's returning to her. The vision was void of his presence. In her innermost spirit, she knew he wouldn't be back.

Chapter Nine

Mike's house lay six miles out of town on a dirt offshoot from Vista Chino Drive. He'd bought the place cheap when he'd come to the desert and saw it more as an investment than a home.

Throwing a cloud of dust and sand up behind his car, he slid around the last bend and came to a halt opposite the arches framing his front porch. The Spanish-style house had been the dream of an erstwhile jojoba bean farmer. When the bean fields had failed to produce, the dream had died and Mike had bought the property, big house, sheds and all.

Mike switched off the Toyota's engine and sat perfectly still, letting the dust settle. He looked at the red tile roof outlined against the night sky, the arched windows and the wrought-iron fencing around his small, unkempt lawn. It was a nice enough place, he supposed, if you didn't care one way or the other where you slept. It was clean and warm—luxuries he hadn't enjoyed when he'd lived on the streets at sixteen, doing odd jobs to pay for the necessities of life.

Shuddering, he climbed out of the car. Amy had him re-membering far too much, far too often. That part of his life lay behind him. It was over. Done.

Even if I could change it now, he mused, walking to the door and unlocking it, I wouldn't know where to begin.

The living room was dark, but Mike crossed it without concern that he'd bump into furniture. There wasn't any. Unfurnished when he'd bought it nearly two years before, the spacious house remained a hollow shell of its former self. Of necessity, Mike had added a refrigerator to the self-contained kitchen and a bed and dresser to the room where he slept. The only luxury he allowed himself was in the den, a place he referred to as his office.

Stopping in the kitchen, he opened the refrigerator and helped himself to a beer. Carrying it with him to the bed-room, he undressed, decided he wouldn't be able to sleep if he tried and pulled on faded jeans, a gray sweatshirt and old deck shoes.

"This is a nice place," he muttered, as if seeing it through different eyes. "Not exactly homey, but passably nice."

He finally settled down in the den. Propping his feet on one of the two leather side chairs, he leaned back in the other and stared at the little white bumps in the acoustic-tile ceiling.

He took a swallow of beer. The ceiling at the halfway house had been made of the same stuff. He tipped up the can. So had the one above his bed at Kovacik's.

Kovacik's. Humpf. It had been—Lord—at least fifteen years since he'd last seen Betty Kovacik, and he wondered if her salt-and-pepper hair had ever turned entirely gray. He chuckled. A few more kids like him entrusted to her care and he figured it had to be snow white by now!

She'd written, of course. Betty was like that. And she'd sent the packet of belongings he'd left behind when he'd decided that a foster home as straight as Kovacik's was no place for him and had taken to the streets.

Mike got to his feet. His memories were like a dormant volcano. Long quiet, they'd begin to boil beneath the surface then erupt startlingly into the present. Unwanted and uncalled for, those memories were nonetheless there, bubbling faster and faster before spewing into the light of his consciousness.

Pacing, he shook his head. Amy Alexander had done this to him. Amy and her questions. Amy, with her loving nature and attitudes about life and families. Well, she'd change her mind fast enough if she knew the truth about Ray, the man she worshipped as the perfect father.

"But she won't," Mike declared. "Because I'm not ever going to tell her."

He crushed the empty can and tossed it into the wastebasket beside his desk. Betty would approve of the way he'd turned out, he decided. She'd been the one who always insisted he was a good person at heart.

And he'd been just as certain he wasn't. He'd given that poor woman fits toward the end. Between his running away and failure to apply himself at school, there wasn't much she could honestly praise him for. Yet she'd always found something, hadn't she?

Smiling, Mike rested on the edge of his desk, folded his arms across his chest and shook his head. Poor old Betty. She'd been just another pain-in-the-neck foster parent to him at the time. Looking back he could see how hard she'd tried to reach him, how long-suffering yet necessarily firm she'd been through it all.

The padded manila mailer she'd sent through the juvenile authorities had been waiting for him when he'd gotten out of the army. Many times he'd been ready to throw it away, unopened, but something had stayed his hand. Where had he put it? Mike paused. It had to be either in the garage or stuck away in one of the closets.

He opted for the easiest place to begin searching, crossed to the closet and located the envelope in a cardboard box tucked behind an old tennis racket and some souvenir beer mugs he'd collected overseas when he was in the service.

The ink on the yellow envelope was faded, the amount of postage long obsolete. Hefting it, he turned it over in his hands.

Mike stood for several minutes deciding whether to open Betty's gift. Knowing her, it contained the last of the concrete evidence of his troubled childhood. Curiosity had failed to motivate him to open the envelope when he'd first received it. Now, maybe it was time.

Seating himself at his desk, he pulled apart the staples holding the top flaps together and spilled the contents onto the blotter in front of him. Slowly, he spread the pile with his hands, reverently touching all that was left of the unwanted boy he'd once been.

There was a photograph of the McPhersons he'd not recalled having, some old report cards with grades best forgotten, the key chain Betty had given him on that last Christmas—she'd promised he could learn to drive in her car if his grades improved—and assorted Polaroids of the other boys she had looked after. Mike chuckled. He couldn't remember any of their names.

There was also a letter sealed in a plain white envelope amid the clutter. The handwriting was definitely Betty's. Mike plucked it from the pile and opened it.

"Dear Michael," it began. "I hope and pray you'll one day read this and be able to understand."

Mike laid the letter on the desk as he continued to read.

"When you left, you told me you didn't want any of the personal effects I'm sending you, but then you were very young and upset. You thought life had dealt you a terrible blow. Well, I don't dispute that. But now that you're older, perhaps you can also see that you've grown strong because of your trials. You'll be a fine man someday, and maybe then you'll wish you had the things in this package.

"I loved you, Michael," Betty wrote. "You and all the 'bad' boys they sent me. I only pray I was able to make some small difference in your life. Love, Mrs. K."

Mike thoughtfully folded the letter. Returning most of the contents to the envelope he picked up the key chain, tossed it into the air, caught it and slipped it into his pocket. Quite a lady, that Mrs. K., he mused, smiling. He'd have to look her up someday soon. She always *did* like knowing when she was right.

Mike rubbed the back of his neck. It was late, but sleep still was out of the question. He had been shirking the job lately though, thanks to his obsession with Amy's mystery. If he went to the office at least he could get some work done, update the files, so the night wouldn't be a total waste.

Grabbing his keys off the dresser, he flipped the lock on the front door and headed for his car.

Slowly, Amy walked to the sink, poured her cold coffee down the drain and unplugged her coffee maker. How long had she sat there, alone in the stillness? She didn't know, nor did she care. Mike had left, and the light had gone out of her life. It was as simple as that.

Feeling a sudden chill, she wrapped her arms around her waist. Why couldn't she have fallen in love with a man who was ready to love her in return? Why hadn't she found herself drawn to that undergraduate student, John Lasswell, or her new waiter, Bob Lee? Both were personable men, and each had expressed a romantic interest in her. So why was Mike Dixon the one man who made her pulse quicken, who banished all thoughts of other suitors from her mind?

Darned if she knew. Nothing in her life had made much sense since she'd stumbled on the fact she was adopted. Not that she could blame all her unrest on Mike. That wouldn't be fair. He had, however, done his part to contribute seriously to the problem.

You know what your trouble is? she asked herself. You expect to be able to order your life into neat little categories just like you do when you manage operations at Marino's. Amy shook her head. Well, life isn't like that.

The dinner dishes that Mike had stacked by the sink still waited for attention, but Amy didn't crave busywork the way she craved affection. She could feel herself in Mike's arms, smell his after-shave, sense the strength of his character, the depth of his hidden feelings for her. She remembered how he had seemed to be trying to bridge the chasms between them.

Yes, he'd pulled away. He'd run from her, from the commitment she wanted. Yet deep down, Amy knew he'd belonged to her and she to him almost from the start.

He'd also been sensitive to her loneliness, she reminded herself. Long before she'd had the guts to acknowledge how truly alone she felt since her father's death, Mike had seen her need and given her unconditional love in the guise of Seymour.

That silly cat had gotten to her, too. Once again she looked forward to coming home in the evenings because she could always count on a greeting overflowing with affection. His antics made her laugh, no matter how tired she was or how trying Alonzo had been. Sometimes Seymour's escapades were so perfect, so attuned to her moods, it seemed as if he were psychic.

But right now, he was not providing the TLC she needed. Amy glanced at the cat's bed. It was empty. She tiptoed into the living room expecting to find him sound asleep in one of the forbidden places he loved. She'd tried in vain to teach him that the furniture was taboo, but so far all she'd managed to do was make a game of catching him in the act of snoozing on the upholstery.

Flicking on the light, Amy peeked over the back of the wing chair, one of his favorites. The seat cushion was soft, and he liked to push his way between it and the padded back, making a little nest behind the throw pillows.

She jerked a blue-patterned pillow into the air. That would startle Seymour and serve him right. Only he wasn't there, either. Puzzled, Amy hugged the pillow close.

Enough of this game, she decided. It was late, and she was exhausted. "Seymour? Come here, you little stinker. Where are you?"

Amy padded barefoot across the dining room, checking the seats of her dining table chairs. Seymour also liked to hide there, batting at her like a mountain lion after its prey as she passed. His soft paws never injured, his claws were always sheathed, and Amy usually used one finger to duel with him for a few seconds before laughing and hoisting him in her arms where he purred contentedly as long as she held him.

"Seymour?" Making a face, she stood with her hands on her hips. "Seymour, come here. If you do, I'll let you sleep on the bed tonight, I promise." She bent to look under the table. "Seymour?"

Again she felt a chill, a breeze that didn't belong in the house. When she'd first sensed the cold she'd assumed it was a result of her active imagination and Mike's absence. Now, she looked for a more logical cause for the goose bumps on her arms.

The door! Her gaze fastened on the front door. She hadn't walked Mike out, and apparently he'd forgotten her warnings about the tricky latch.

Amy's voice grew frantic. "Seymour!" She crossed quickly to the door, her hand on the knob.

With one foot on the porch, one still inside, she peered into the darkness. "Seymour!" No yellow and white cat appeared. No answering meow echoed in the night air.

Breathing rapidly, Amy entered the house, closing the door securely. If Seymour wasn't already outside, she wasn't going to give him the chance to escape. And if he was, what then? He didn't know how to fend for himself in the world. If a car didn't get him he'd probably starve!

Amy wiped salty tears from her eyes. This was no time for panic. If her sweet pet was to survive she'd have to keep her head. Think! What now?

A thorough sweep of the house, she reasoned. And *two* people could do a better job than one. Mike was supposed to be the expert at finding lost souls, and he was the one who'd left the door open. He could just come and help her.

With trembling hands Amy opened the phone book, her finger tracing the column until she had read all the Dixons. Mike's home number was unlisted. She fumbled in her purse for his card.

No one would be in the office at three in the morning, of course, but at least she could leave a message and Mike would learn about Seymour first thing in the morning.

This is silly, Amy argued to herself as she dialed. Why involve Mike?

Because he's the only one in your life you want to call, she answered. He's the one who matters. He's the one who showed you he understood by getting you Seymour in the first place. He deserves to hear he's lost.

The telephone rang three times before the recorded message on the answering machine kicked in. Amy listened while she rehearsed the calm, sensible message she intended to leave. When the tone sounded and she began to speak, all her logic fled and she spoke as if to Mike himself.

"It's Amy," she blurted. "When you left, you didn't close the door." That was awful, Amy, her conscience complained. Fix it.

"I'm not saying it's your fault, honest, I'm not," she added, "but Seymour's gone! I can't find him anywhere."

She paused for a breath. "I tried to phone you at home but I didn't have the number. I'm going to search the house. Beyond that I don't know what to do. I just thought, if *two* of us looked..."

A loud beep cut her off. A timer. The darned thing was on a timer! She'd fully intended to end her message by telling Mike not to worry, that she'd call again and let him know if the cat had turned up, but there hadn't been enough time on the stupid machine.

Her hand was poised over the telephone. Spare time was what she didn't have if poor Seymour was lost outside. There would be plenty of opportunity to dial Mike's number before his office opened in the morning. Right now, she had a lost cat to find.

Amy pulled on a warm fleece jacket and slipped her feet into flat shoes. If Seymour was hiding *in* the house, he'd be fine. Oh, he might get into all kinds of mischief, but he'd be safe enough.

However, if he'd really left, as she suspected, he was in danger. The best thing to do was to scour the neighborhood first.

Mike saw the flashing red light on his answering machine when he entered his office and chose to ignore it. Whatever the problem was, it would keep until Marie got there at eight and sorted it out.

Pulling three current files, he took them to his desk, spread them out and stared at them. Two were searches for spouses who had left town to avoid paying alimony. The third was the wandering husband case he'd been on the night he'd fixed the mulligan stew for Amy.

Amy's was the case he should be concentrating on, Mike told himself. He knew he wouldn't rest until he'd done his best for her whether he told her about it or not. As he saw it, his biggest problem would be gathering the pertinent information without her knowledge.

With a deep breath, Mike leaned back and laced his fingers together behind his head. Here he sat, thinking of Amy again. There was no end to it.

Disgusted with himself, he reached for the dial of the answering machine, turned it to playback and picked up a pencil while he listened to the whir of the rewinding tape. Maybe the caller could provide enough stimulus to take his mind off the ache in his loins.

Before she'd finished uttering her name, Mike knew who had called him. He sat bolt upright and turned up the volume. Damn. Amy needed him. Seymour was gone, and it looked like it was *his* fault.

The tape was still running when Mike hit the sidewalk at a run, jumped into his car and headed for Calle El Segundo fast enough to get himself arrested if there had been a police car along his route.

Mike's loud knocks on her door didn't raise Amy, but Evangeline Norton did appear.

"What's all the noise?" she demanded.

"Amy. Ms. Alexander," Mike said. "Do you know if she's home?"

"Doubt it," the old woman said tersely. "Heard her hollerin' for that damned cat of hers and then the door slammed. Suppose she went lookin' for it."

Mike glanced quickly from side to side, up and down the empty street. "Alone? Now?" Dear Lord, it wasn't safe for a pretty woman to be wandering the streets alone at four in the morning no matter *where* she lived.

"Sure, alone," Evangeline told him. "I wasn't about to volunteer to run around in the dark with her. She lives by herself, you know."

"I know." Mike started down the steps. "I don't suppose you saw which way she went?"

"Might have. She was sure makin' enough noise."

"Well?" He stifled the urge to return to the porch and give the woman a good shake. "Which way?"

A bony finger pointed toward the north. "That way, for starters, but it's been nearly an hour. No tellin' where she might be by now."

"Thanks," Mike muttered, jogging to his car. Sure, he cared about Seymour, but Amy's safety came first. And where she was at this hour of the morning he could only guess.

Driving slowly, he headed down the street, trying to think as he imagined Amy would. It was impossible. She'd sounded so distressed, so agitated on the recording, he had no idea what was going through her head. He only hoped she had enough sense to stick to the best lighted streets.

It was close to ten minutes later before he spotted the white of her dress and the bright yellow fleece jacket she'd worn over it. She was bending down, shining the beam of a small flashlight beneath a shrub in a yard. Easing the Toyota to the curb, he rolled down the passenger window to call to her.

Amy sensed a car slowing down behind her. She tensed. If whoever it was accosted her, where could she escape? Her eyes darted to the iron gates across the driveway of the house she'd been examining. Running that way was no good unless she could vault the fence faster than her pursuer!

She'd taken a deep breath, preparing to scream, when she heard Mike's familiar voice. Flooded with relief she shined her light at the car.

"Oh, thank goodness." Approaching, she leaned in the open window. "I thought you were one of the bad guys."

"I could have been," he said brusquely. "Listen. I want to apologize for the way I snapped at you earlier. You didn't do anything to deserve treatment like that."

"I'm sorry, too," Amy said. "It wasn't my intention to pry into your life. The question seemed natural, and I asked it before I thought."

"Okay. We were both wrong. Now, get in."

"But . . . Seymour's lost. I have to find him." Her voice broke. "Oh, Mike. What am I going to do if I don't?"

Reaching across, he flipped the door handle to admit her. "Just get in. We can do this better together."

What a relief. "That's what *I* thought," Amy said. "I tried to call you at home to ask for your help but your number is unlisted." She frowned. "Wait a minute. How did you know to come looking for me?"

"I went to the office."

"In the middle of the night?" She settled herself into the car seat and shut the door.

"I couldn't sleep."

Amy laid her head on the headrest and smiled. It was hardly surprising that Mike had insomnia. What did shock and please her, though, was how freely he'd admitted it. Maybe there was hope for their relationship yet.

Chapter Ten

Amy didn't object when Mike brought his car to a halt in her driveway. He was the expert. She'd gladly follow whatever search procedures he suggested. Together, they walked to the front porch.

"I think I locked myself out," she said.

"Figures. You were sure upset when you left that message."

"I'm sorry if I sounded like I was accusing you."

He shook his head to dismiss her apology. "I'll go around and let myself in the back. You wait here."

"Okay." As he started away she stopped him with a hand on his arm. "Mike, thanks for coming to help. You don't know how much having you here means to me. I really appreciate it."

He laid his hand over hers. "Good Lord, woman, your fingers are freezing!"

"I hadn't really noticed. I've been too worried."

"Come on, before you catch pneumonia." Gathering her to him with an arm around her waist, Mike whisked her off the porch and around the house. Opening the back door with the key hidden in the flowerpot, he replaced the key and ushered Amy into her warm kitchen.

"Make something hot to drink," he ordered. "Then we'll turn this place inside out till we find Seymour, okay?"

"I'm afraid he's not here," Amy said, plugging in her coffee maker to reheat the hours-old coffee rather than bother with a fresh batch when she was so rattled. "He didn't come when I called him." Her lower lip began to tremble, and she turned away to hide her emotions from Mike.

He wasn't fooled. Coming up behind her he gently grasped her upper arms. "Don't worry, honey. We'll find him."

His tenderness was enough to push her emotions over the edge, and she felt her tears begin to trickle down. "We have to," she said, turning to look at him. "We just *have* to."

Wiping away a drop from her cheek, Mike smiled to console her. "Well, if we don't I'll buy you another kitten. Okay?"

Amy stared at him as if he'd just proposed they join forces to commit a murder. Her jaw dropped. "Wh-what?"

"I said I'll get you another cat."

She sniffled, trying to control the weeping that threatened to erupt. "No! Don't even talk like that. I don't want another cat. I want Seymour."

"I know you do, honey," Mike said. "But in case we don't find him . . ."

Amy pressed her fingertips to her lips. "Please. Stop."

"Don't get so upset," he said calmly. "You liked having Seymour around, so I'll replace him for you."

Amy reached for a tissue, blew her nose and faced Mike squarely. "You think one cat is just like any other, don't you?"

"It is." It was hard to keep the emotion off his face, but Mike managed. Hell, he was attached to Seymour, too, but letting Amy know that wouldn't help.

"And I suppose you classify people the same way?" she asked, grabbing a second tissue to blot at her eyes. "Is that why it doesn't matter to you whether or not our friendship lasts?"

She saw no reaction from him so she continued. "Well, it matters to me, Mike Dixon. There isn't one living being in this whole world who's not unique. We can't be replaced like a used-up tube of toothpaste, you know."

He reached for her, touching her arm. "You're blowing this all out of proportion."

"Am I?" She stripped off her jacket and tossed it onto a chair, then led the way into the living room.

Mike followed. "Yes. I didn't mean that Seymour could be replaced. I just thought the promise of another cat might cheer you up."

Seeing his reasoning, Amy allowed him to approach closer. "There's only one Seymour," she said. "And there's only one you, one me. None of us may be perfect—" she began to smile through the remnants of her tears "—although I'd venture to say I'm closer to it than either you or Seymour are."

"Thanks."

"Don't mention it." Looking into Mike's eyes she studied him carefully. "But perfect or not, we're special human beings, just like Seymour's a special cat."

"I know that."

Amy cupped his cheek in her palm, her gaze tender. "Do you? I wonder."

As Mike looked at the concern reflected in her misty eyes, he realized how much he truly loved her and marveled at all the offers of affection he'd probably thrown away in the past. Amy understood what was important in life a lot better than he ever would.

"Have I told you how much you remind me of Betty Kovacik?" he finally asked.

Casting him a sidelong glance, Amy withdrew her touch and cocked her head. "Who's she?"

"Just an old friend, so don't bother ordering her a ticket to Siberia."

"Okay." Relaxing, Amy took Mike's hand. "I'm sorry if I gave you a bad time. I feel responsible for what's happened, and it's made me a little crazy."

"A little?" Mike was smiling, now, and his fingers closed around Amy's.

"Okay. A lot."

"Granted. But why feel responsible? You didn't leave the door open. I did."

"Yes, but Seymour was mine. It was my responsibility to feed, house and care for him. The guilt I felt when I saw that open door was awful!"

"Even though you knew you hadn't been the one to leave it that way?"

"Sure."

He frowned. "I don't understand."

"I don't either, exactly," Amy confessed. "It has to be a bit like being a parent, though. I mean, there you are, an adult used to looking after only yourself, and all of a sudden a helpless baby's entire existence is dependent upon you. What a frightening thought that must be."

Pensive, Mike slipped his arm around her shoulders. "You're right. I'd never given it much consideration before, but I do see what you're trying to say."

Squeezing her to him he placed a light kiss on the top of her head, more to reassure himself than for Amy's benefit. She *was* right. More right than she could possibly know. Her abstract ramblings brushed dangerously near to the awful secret Ray had taken to his grave with him. If what Mike suspected was true, there was a woman, probably very much like Amy, who still wrongly blamed herself for the loss of her infant daughter all those years ago.

Holding Amy close, he tucked her head beneath his chin and stared absently across the room. "If it tears you up like this to lose Seymour, it must really be traumatic to have a child disappear."

"I can't think of anything worse," Amy said softly.

Mike shook his head. "No, honey. Neither can I."

"You ought to go home," Amy told Mike when she saw him yawn. "We've been through the whole house twice."

"I know." Amy was seated on the edge of the bed. He sank down beside her and ran his fingers through his hair. "I was positive he was here."

"Well, he isn't," she said flatly. Her hand caressed Mike's shoulder. "I'll advertise for him in the newspaper and put signs up in all the stores that have public bulletin boards."

"Let me offer a reward. It's the least I can do."

"All right. In the meantime, you'd better go home and try to get some sleep."

Mike chuckled as he checked his watch. "Too late. My alarm clock is set to wake me in thirty minutes."

"In that case..." Stooping and grabbing his feet, Amy lifted them, swiveled his body to the side and gave him a gentle push that landed him flat on his back on the bed.

The soft comforter was a pastel floral design. Ruffled shams covered the pillows. The bed's obviously feminine look vividly reminded him where he was. With a sheepish look he started to get to his feet. "I shouldn't be in your bed."

"Why not? You're alone."

He blushed crimson, the color rising up his neck and suffusing his cheeks. "That's true."

"Then what's your problem? I'll admit the spread is probably not macho enough for you but with your eyes closed you won't see it."

"I wasn't objecting to your taste in decorating," he insisted. "I just felt awkward about being in your bed."

"Nonsense. You wouldn't have missed so much sleep if you hadn't been helping me." Reaching over him for a pillow to tuck under his head she grabbed the nearest sham by its ruffle. "Here."

Tenderly he closed his fingers around her wrist to stop her fussing. It would be so easy to pull her down beside him—so right to be with her. Their time together, looking for Seymour, had magnified his feelings for her until they were impossible to deny. The rest was only natural.

"Amy, I ..."

At that precise moment her jaw slackened, her eyes opening wider than Mike had ever seen them and focusing past his shoulder. She screamed, and the pillow went sailing into the air!

Instinctively, he rolled to the floor, carrying her with him, and placed his body protectively between Amy and whatever it was that had frightened her so. His weight and quick movements knocked her breathless.

"What is it?" Mike demanded, stretched out over her. "Tell me!"

Amy could only gesture, point and gasp.

When Mike lifted himself high enough to crouch and peer over the edge of the bed he came face to face with a very startled Seymour. "Well, I'll be damned."

"You'll be more than that if you don't get off me," Amy threatened. "I think you broke me in half."

"I'm sorry." Quickly rising, he took her hands and pulled her to her feet. "When you yelled I thought there was a rattlesnake in bed with me. This is the desert, you know. Those things can happen out here."

"For a second, that was exactly what I thought," Amy told him, brushing at her skirt with trembling fingers. "All I saw at first was Seymour's tail." She pressed both hands to her throat. "He scared me to death!"

"Your scream did a fairly good job on me, too." He'd grasped her shoulders. "You okay now?"

Amy nodded. "I think I'll live."

"Good." Mike turned, lifting the unnerved cat in his arms and ruffling the fur around its ears. "If it's any consolation, I think we scared Seymour more than he scared us. The hair on his back is still standing on end!"

"It serves him right." Leaning closer, Amy kissed the cat on the bridge of his nose. "We'll never forgive him, will we, Mike?"

"Nope. He should have to take us out to breakfast to make up for our long night."

"Unfortunately, Seymour is unemployed at the moment, so that's out," Amy said. "However, as his guardian, I feel it's my duty to provide the things he can't."

Smiling sweetly, she chucked the cat under the chin and gazed at the precious man holding him. Mike's eyes had dark shadows under them, his hair was tousled, and coarse stubble had begun to show on his chin. In short, he looked wonderful.

Careful not to disturb his hold on Seymour, Amy took Mike's arm. "So, how do you like your eggs, Mr. Dixon?"

Mike started to make excuses then changed his mind. He'd had a hell of a night—as a matter of fact, the past few months hadn't been all that easy—and he was ready and willing to share a peaceful breakfast with the two favorite people in his life, Amy and Seymour.

"Over hard," Mike said. "I can't stand runny yolks."

"Me, either. They mess up the toast."

"Toast? We're having toast, too?" he teased. "Let's not get carried away."

Giggling, Amy waited until they'd reached the relative safety of her kitchen before she said what had popped into her mind. "If we didn't get carried away in the bedroom when you jumped on me, I don't think we have to worry about the effects of eating toast together."

"I thought of it," Mike said.

"Of the effects of eating toast?"

"No. Of getting carried away with you."

"You did?" Her voice was barely audible. "When?"

Constantly was the first word that came to mind but he decided to be a little less accurate. "It doesn't matter. The important thing is, I didn't do anything about it."

She'd opened her mouth to reply when the serious expression on Mike's face stopped her. Their joking time was over. If she pressed him now, the result might not be what she wanted.

And what *do* you want? Amy asked herself.

Just what I've got, she answered, looking over at Mike as he put fresh food down for Seymour. A family.

Mrs. Norton was peeking out through a slit in her curtains when Mike finally bid Amy goodbye. Judging from what little Mike and Amy could see, lecherous thoughts were racing through the busybody's mind. Sniffing derogatorily the older woman released her hold on the curtain. It fell into place but not so tightly that she couldn't still peer through the crack.

Laughing under his breath, Mike cocked his head toward the next door neighbor's window. "We have an audience."

"Usually." Amy was tolerant of Evangeline's habits.

"Does she often see men leaving your place after breakfast?"

"You know she doesn't."

"Then suppose we give her her money's worth?"

"Something to write home about?" Amy was grinning broadly.

"Right. A cheap thrill."

"Speak for yourself, Mike Dixon," she taunted. Stepping closer she looked into his eyes. "What exactly did you have in mind?"

"This."

His arms captured Amy and pulled her close as his mouth descended to claim hers in a demanding kiss that sent sparks coursing through her until she was dizzy with pleasure. Sliding her hands up and over Mike's shoulders she wrapped her arms around his neck and returned the kiss in the only way she could—with every fiber of her being.

Breathing raggedly, he lifted his head to gaze at her. "How was that?"

Too darned short, Amy contended, deciding to try to prolong their theatrical goodbye. "I don't think we've shocked her enough," she said as her eyes darted to the split in the curtains. "She hasn't fogged up the windowpane yet."

"Oh. Well, in that case..." Bending Amy back over his arm like Valentino, Mike rained kisses over her cheeks, eyelids, neck and finally into the smooth valley between her breasts at the scooping neckline of her dress.

Amy had gasped and begun to giggle when he'd first laid her over backward. Now, as he kissed her, she sobered. It was evident Mike was feeling the same seriousness. His teasing, flamboyant kisses had become sensual explorations, and she was certain, if he didn't stop soon, they'd give poor Mrs. Norton more of a show than either of them had bargained for.

Abruptly, Mike righted her. "I think that's enough," he said, his voice gruff, his complexion ruddy.

Straightening, she smoothed her dress into place. "I agree."

"Thanks for breakfast. I'd better get home and clean up or I'll be late for work."

Amy's hand touched his flushed cheek and traveled down the firm line of his jaw. "You do need a shave."

"Among other things," he said, arching one eyebrow.

She wanted desperately to ask him when she'd see him again, but past experience had taught her the folly of a question like that. The next move was Mike's. Amy almost wept with joy when he made it.

"Will you be free this weekend?" Making plans for Saturday or Sunday would give him nearly a week in which to work on Amy's case and pull the loose ends together. He hoped it would be long enough.

"Of course, I'll be free." She couldn't keep the joy out of her voice or her expression.

"Good."

He grasped her hands. Thinking about solving her case he glanced toward his Toyota. A recent clear photograph of her was one of the things Mike knew he'd need to add to her growing file.

"Listen. I have a camera in the car," he said. "Would you mind if I snapped a picture of you?"

"Well, no." Tossing her head, Amy flipped her hair over her shoulders. "But how about taking it when I haven't been up all night? I mean, my hair needs combing and I'm sure I haven't had any lipstick on since dinner."

"You look fine."

"But..." She watched him hurry to his car, reach beneath the passenger's seat and withdraw a small black camera. On the way back to the porch he fitted it with a larger lens. The man was serious!

"Look, Mike," she said quickly. "If you want a picture of me let me give you a professional portrait I had done a few years ago."

"I can take that, too." Widening his stance for balance, Mike leaned back, adjusted the focus on his camera and snapped the shutter once before he added, "But I also want a current shot. The older you look, the better."

"Older?" Amy's hands flew up like a shield between her and the camera. "Thanks a bunch."

Mike's laughter was making the camera jiggle too much to be of any use, and he lowered it. "Maybe I should have said mature?"

"That's not a whole lot better," she complained. "What do you want a picture for, anyway?"

"I'm a sucker for a pretty face," he said.

She wrinkled her nose.

"Cute. Now, step out into the sunlight for me. I want to catch the way your hair sparkles."

"It does?" Amy felt more like she was six years old than twenty-three. Of all the times to want to take her picture! Didn't Mike know about a woman's pride?

"Smile."

She tried to, but when he laughed at her pained expression Amy refused to stand still for any more shots. Bouncing down the porch steps she took the camera from him. "Okay. Your turn."

No one had photographed him since his mandatory ID picture, and he swore he couldn't recall the last time anyone had actually wanted a likeness of him. Amy's request took him by surprise.

"No. Come on," he argued, reaching for the camera.

Amy wouldn't be deterred. "Hush. You got your way. Now it's my turn."

Pointing at the lens as she backed away, Mike was babbling something about focusing. Amy ignored him. After her college photography class, operating the simple camera was a cinch.

"You won't get anything good if you don't refocus carefully each time," Mike was saying. "I'm telling you."

She was dancing around in front of him, catching the play of light and shadow on his face as the morning sun rose in the eastern sky. The pictures would be great! "Smile."

"Nonsense," Mike grumbled, reaching for the camera and capturing it behind her back because his reach was longer than hers. "You didn't get one acceptable shot."

"Wanna bet?"

"Sure." Turning the camera over in his hands he replaced the lens cap. "How much of a bet did you have in mind?"

"Oh, not money," Amy assured him. "How about dinner?"

"Where? The Pines?"

"That's too easy," Amy said. "Tell you what. If your pictures are better than mine, I'll cook here. But if my pictures of you are the best on the roll, then you'll cook for me at your place."

He shook his head in the negative. "You don't even know where I live."

"True. But I trust you. And I'm willing to go wherever it is you live. That's no problem."

"No, I don't suppose it would be for you. I don't have any furniture, though."

"So? I'll bring a chair. How about it? Is it a bet?"

Mike scowled. "You seem awfully sure of yourself."

"I'm an optimist. Besides, why worry? You told me my pictures wouldn't be any good if I didn't do it your way."

"They won't be, and I'm not worried." He chuckled at the enthusiastic look on her face. "Okay. It's a deal."

Putting the camera in the car, Mike picked up a small spiral note pad, wrote on it, tore out the sheet and brought it to Amy. "Here's my home address and phone number in case you need to reach me again, and Marie can beep me through my office phone. I'll always be accessible, one way or another."

"You don't have to do this, you know," she said quietly. "I wasn't fishing when I said I didn't know where you lived."

"I know that. Actually, I live on a bean farm." Waiting for her predictable reaction, Mike smiled.

"Do you have a good crop?" she asked, returning his grin.

"Nary a bean."

"That's too bad. A bean farmer without beans is in deep trouble."

Laughing, Mike gazed lovingly at Amy. Her hair was mussed, her beautiful dress wrinkled, her eyes the color of the sky above, and there was a faint dusting of freckles across her nose that made her look a bit mischievous and totally enchanting. He was in trouble, all right, but it had nothing to do with beans.

Amy was working at Marino's when she next heard from Mike. Marissa took the call, pretending to swoon when she handed it off to Amy.

"I hope I didn't disturb you," Mike said.

"Not at all." Amy purposely scowled at Marissa, sending her back to work by gesturing wildly and pointing to the dining room. "Do you have the pictures back already?"

"Yes. I took them to a one-day developer."

The ensuing period of silence went on so long Amy stepped in to fill the gap. "Well? How are they?"

"Fine. *All* of them," he said dryly. "We'll probably have to call in an independent judging organization to decide who wins our bet."

"I don't mind." No matter whose pictures were best, she and Mike would be together as a result. The way Amy saw it, she won either way.

"The reason I called," he said slowly, deliberately, "was to tell you I'll be out of town on business for a few days."

Amy gripped the receiver tightly. "How long?"

"Not long. Just until I complete my search or until I see that it's one of those instances where things are best left unsettled. I should be home by the weekend, like we'd planned."

She decided he sounded odd, like he might be hiding something. "This trip doesn't have anything to do with my adoption, does it? Because if it does—"

"No. Don't worry about that."

"Then what's wrong? You sound like you don't want to go at all," she observed. "Can't you get someone else to do it in your place?"

Mike sighed. "Normally, I could. But in this case, I'm afraid I may have to bend the rules a bit, and I don't want to put another investigator in a bad position with the law."

"But what about you? Surely no case is worth taking risks like that."

"This one is," he told her solemnly. "I'll be as cautious as I can, but this particular investigation is too important to drop. I have to see it through."

He'd already said too much, Mike told himself. Why was it so hard for him to lie to her, even for her own good? Amy wasn't questioning his explanation of his upcoming trip, but she soon would unless he broke off their conversation.

"I have to go," he said tersely. "I'll call you as soon as I get home. All right?"

"Of course it's all right." She knew he was worried about the case he was on and didn't want to add to his concern by expressing her disappointment. "Just promise me you'll be careful?"

"I promise," was the last thing she heard him say.

Chapter Eleven

Mike caught up with Lieutenant Bob Finch at a sidewalk hot-dog stand near the fountain in Balboa Park. The San Diego weather was cooler than what Mike had left behind in Palm Springs, and he was glad he'd had the foresight to wear a sweater under his windbreaker.

Lovers cavorted along the wide lip of the park's enormous fountain, and Mike smiled, thinking of Amy when he saw a laughing young man lift his girl into the air and threaten to dunk her in the pool beneath the plumes of spray while she squealed and clung tightly to him.

Finch had a passion for the chili dogs served in the park, and when he wasn't in his office at noon, Mike had taken the chance he'd find him at their old haunt. Predictable as always, Finch was there.

He wasn't exactly thrilled to see Mike. "Geez, Dixon. Where did you come from?" He snorted derisively. "You're gonna give me indigestion."

Cocking his head toward the messy concoction Finch had nearly consumed, Mike raised one eyebrow. "If you get indigestion, blame *that* thing, not me. Besides, I had to come. I need your help.''

"No way.''

"Come on, Bob. Just this once?''

"Once, my Aunt Fanny. I left strict orders. Who blabbed and told you where I was?''

"My stomach.'' Mike bought himself a chili dog and a soft drink just like Finch's and sat down on the white-painted bench next to him. "We used to come here together, remember?''

"Yeah, I remember.'' Wiping his mouth with a paper napkin, the middle-aged lieutenant eyed Mike. "You still on the same case?''

Mike nodded. "But never mind that. How's Nancy and the boy? Frankie, isn't it?''

"Yeah.'' The lieutenant smiled. "You ought to settle down and get married, Mike. It's great if you find the right woman.''

"Not me,'' Mike said flatly, decisively. "I've always been a loner, and it's too late to change my ways now. Besides, where would I find a woman who'd put up with me, huh?'' He smiled. "So, go on. Tell me about Frankie.''

"Ah, he's some kid, that one. I help coach his little league team.''

"I'll bet he's proud to have his dad so interested in him, too. Does Nancy watch the games?'' Mike took a bite of his hot dog, licking the chili that started to drip over the side of the bun.

"Boy, does she. You should hear her scream when he gets a hit!''

Lowering his voice, Mike focused his eyes on his lunch but his concentration was all on Bob Finch. "I remember when Frankie was born. You and Nancy were sure proud.''

"No kidding. That kid is everything to us.'' Finch laughed.

"Can you imagine how Nancy would have reacted if Frankie had been stolen from the hospital?"

Finch's head snapped up, his eyes glaring. "That was a low blow, Dixon."

"Okay. Don't think about how your wife would have suffered. And be sure not to consider what both your lives would be like without your son. You wouldn't want to know, even years later, what had happened to him, would you? He'd be a lost chapter in your lives, so you'd never remember him."

"Bull." Finch was staring into his cup of soda, swirling it around so the pieces of ice clinked together.

"The hospital stonewalled me," Mike said. Resting his elbows on his knees, he mirrored the lieutenant's position. "They said they'd settled a suit for damages years ago and refused to give out any information."

"You can get the birth certificates."

"With a judge's order, but it takes time, and besides, I need a lot more than that to keep from fouling up this incident worse than it already is."

"You in some kind of a hurry?"

"You might put it that way. I want to get this whole mess over with so I can get on with my own life."

"Sounds like you broke the first rule—never let yourself become personally involved."

"It'll pass." Mike drained his drink, still not making eye contact with Finch. "Especially if you help me."

"You tried the newspapers?"

"Sure," Mike said quietly. "The police are to be commended for releasing so few details."

"The babies' first names were listed." Finch finished the soda and began chewing on the ice crystals.

"Their parents' names weren't, though. And neither was the name of the nurse you guys suspected."

"Billingsly."

Mike quickly got out his notepad and wrote the name.

"You're wasting your time with that one," the lieutenant added. "She was cleared."

"You're sure?"

"I'm sure," Finch told him. "The best lead we had was through a guy named Alexis or Anderson or something like that, but he skipped. By the time we got our act together he'd come up with an airtight alibi, thanks to the shady law firm he fronted for."

"Don't play games with me," Mike said. "You know the guy's name was Ray Alexander."

Finch acted amused. "Yeah, it was. I went over the old file again after you had that girl call me." Crumpling his cup, he got to his feet. "Anyway, we couldn't prove anything, and after those first three, no more babies disappeared—at least not around here."

"And you think Alexander was dirty?" Mike watched his expression carefully.

"My gut feelings tell me he was."

Mike stood and disposed of his half-eaten hot dog in a trash receptacle. Suddenly, he'd lost his appetite. He fell into step beside Bob.

The lieutenant wiped his hands and pitched the soiled napkin into the trash. "The thing that puzzles me, though, is why we were never able to pin anything else on the guy. He moved a lot and kept working for the same crooked lawyers, but as far as we could tell, he never helped them acquire another baby."

"And I suppose you checked on the child the Alexanders were raising?"

Finch looked surprised. "Sure. Give us a little credit. She was his, all right. Mrs. Alexander checked into Mercy Hospital downtown, and had that baby herself."

"What?"

"You heard me. I figure it was no coincidence, though, that the other babies disappeared right around the time Mrs.

Alexander was hospitalized to give birth. Her husband's excuse to come and go unquestioned was made to order."

Mike felt every nerve and muscle in his body tensing. "That's impossible, Bob," he said slowly, clearly. "I don't know who the woman in the hospital was, but Martha Alexander had no natural children."

"Of course she did." Frowning, Finch stared at Mike. "Wait a minute. What makes you so *sure* she didn't?"

"I've read her diaries," Mike said. "She's very clear about it."

"Then who was the woman in the hospital who claimed to be Alexander's wife?" the lieutenant asked. "I suppose you're ready to tell me that, too?"

"I'm afraid not," Mike said. "If they did such a good job of covering their tracks then, I don't know how we'd ever prove who she was at this late date."

Finch scowled. "Then what's the point? Why did you disturb my lunch, Dixon? Do you enjoy bugging me?"

"Hardly. I'm out of options, Bob. In normal adoption cases there's at least a paper trail to follow. In this case, I haven't been able to unearth anything."

Reaching into his coat pocket Mike withdrew a small white folder, opened it and chose one of the recent photos of Amy. "This is all I have." He paused. "Were there pictures in the old file?" he asked, cupping his hand around the snapshot.

"Some." Finch had stopped walking and was facing his old friend. "Why?"

"I know it's a long shot, but I thought maybe this girl might look a little like one of those people."

Finch snorted derisively. "You really are desperate, aren't you?"

"Yeah. I am." Opening his hand, Mike displayed Amy's smiling face for the lieutenant. The sunlight had caught in her hair like a golden mantle, and her expression was that of a happy woman gazing at her lover. When this mess was over, Mike intended to keep that particular image of Amy in a frame on his desk.

Startled, Finch poked his finger at the small photo. "Hey! Where did you get that?"

"I took it myself," Mike said, staring at the change in Bob's face. "This is the woman who telephoned you, asking about the case."

"And she matters to you? Give it to me straight, Dixon."

"She matters."

"What's her name?"

Mike paused, never taking his eyes off Finch's face. "Amy Alexander," he said. "Her father and mother were Ray and Martha."

"Geez." The officer's jaw slackened. Thoughtful, he studied Amy's likeness. "Okay. All bets are off. I don't know how he did it, but Alexander apparently put one over on us."

"I'd already figured that he substituted another woman for his wife," Mike said, "but from the look on your face, I'd say there's more to it than that. Am I right?"

"You don't know *how* right," Finch said. "It's a long story, but one of the mothers whose baby disappeared *swore* the hospital had brought her the wrong kid just before it was snatched."

"And?" Mike wanted to grab him to make him talk faster.

"And we weren't able to do any testing or respond to the woman's complaint because the baby disappeared right after she hollered it was the wrong one." He pointed at the snapshot. "*This* woman looks enough like *that* woman to be her twin! You gotta come with me."

"To your office?"

"Yeah. Maybe we can nail Alexander yet." Finch had taken off and was striding rapidly. "You know where he's living now?"

"That's part of the problem," Mike said. "Amy is the only Alexander left. She's all alone."

Slowing his pace, Finch frowned. "So what's the point? What are you trying to do here?"

"Find Amy's real parents," Mike told him. "She's sure she was adopted because Martha Alexander left information to that effect. Now I know why I couldn't find any records."

Finch grasped Mike's arm, stopping him. "Wait a minute. If Alexander went to the trouble of hiring a woman to have a baby legally in his name, why would he jeopardize the plan by switching babies at the last minute?"

"I don't know. We may never know," Mike said soberly. "Maybe there was something wrong with the child. He'd obviously told his wife he'd arranged for them to adopt a newborn infant. He might have panicked and made the switch to save her the pain of raising a kid with genetic problems."

"That's awful farfetched."

"You got a better idea?" Mike asked. "Hell, I don't care why he did it. All I want, now, is to give Amy the chance she deserves to contact her birth mother."

"I can probably help you with that," Bob said. "It'll be worth the hassle if I can figure out how Alexander managed to outwit us."

"No guarantees," Mike warned. "If it might hurt Amy I won't tell you anything I learn."

"You expect me to just waltz in to the station and hand you information with no guarantees?"

"Yes, I do," Mike said.

"And why should I?"

Mike clapped him affectionately on the shoulder. "You'll do it because you know it's right, and because you're a damn good father."

* * *

Marissa wiggled her eyebrows up and down and grinned. "Nobody has to tell me you finally heard from Mike. I can see it on your face."

"He's coming home tonight." Amy sighed. "I never thought one phone call could be so important. I was worried about him."

"What was he doing, chasing criminals or something?"

"He didn't say, specifically. He'd seemed so upset about this case I figured the best thing to do was try to take his mind off it by not mentioning it."

"You *do* know the best way to distract a man from his troubles, don't you?" Marissa asked with a naughty lilt to her voice.

Amy blushed and shot her a shy smile. "Do you ever think of anything else?"

"Ha! Don't look at me so prim and proper, Ms. Alexander. And don't you try to tell me you haven't at least *considered* the same thing." She trailed Amy to her office. "Well?"

"I won't deny I'm attracted to Mike," Amy said.

"Attracted? Give me a break!" Marissa's hands were on her hips, her stance determined. "If you don't admit pretty soon that you love the guy and make up your mind to do something about it, you could lose him."

"But...do what?" Watching her friend, Amy waited for the magic recipe.

Marissa threw her hands into the air, pacing. "I don't know. Something. Anything!" She calmed herself. "Have you told him how you feel?"

"I don't dare." Amy shook her head slowly from side to side as she recalled Mike's reactions to her simplest overtures of friendship. "He won't talk about it, but I suspect he's been deeply hurt in the past. Every time we start to get into a serious discussion he cuts it short."

"Then don't *talk*," Marissa suggested quietly.

"I see what you mean." Thoughtful, she rose and walked to the window. The weather was bright and balmy, the kind of day that gave every part of life a needed springtime lift.

Amy turned to her optimistic friend. "We're meeting at his house for dinner."

"Wonderful! Perfect! You can seduce him there."

"Marissa!"

"I'm serious." She opened the office door to leave. "Give it some thought."

Oh, I will, Amy mused, turning to the window. I will. But as long as Mike hides his past from me, refuses to let me into the private places of his mind, no amount of physical closeness can bridge the gap between us.

Amy sighed in her solitude. I won't hurt you, Mike. I love you. Can't you trust me with your heart?

Mike's house was larger than Amy had imagined it would be. If his familiar Toyota hadn't been parked out front, she might have driven past the place assuming it was deserted. It had plenty of potential to be a lovely home, yet from the look of it, Mike didn't care.

Parking behind the Toyota, Amy stepped out onto the layer of sand that covered the driveway, glad she'd chosen to wear her running shoes and jeans. Straightening her sweater, she paused to look at the house. Empty clay pots hung from hooks between each of the four arches that framed its entrance. Larger vessels, also empty, stood as sentinels beside the carved double doors.

Given a little TLC, the Spanish-style portico could be magnificent, Amy thought. Not all flowering plants were suited to the desert climate, of course, but she could visualize trailing vines and smell the tang of rosemary in the hanging baskets. Lush purple bougainvillea would be perfect to fill the big pots by the door. The effect would be breathtaking.

Amy was standing quietly beneath the overhanging red tile roof when Mike opened the door, startling her. "Oh! Hello."

"I told you it wasn't fancy," he reminded her. The sleeves of his green and white striped sport shirt were rolled up, and he was carrying a dish towel.

"It's beautiful." She started toward the door, then stopped. "I did bring folding chairs and a card table, in case you were serious," Amy said, smiling at Mike. "They're in the trunk."

"It's not quite *that* bare inside," he conceded. "Come on in."

Still awed, she glanced over her shoulder at the expanse of sheltered porch as she entered the house.

"It's well-built and a good investment," Mike said. "That was all I was looking for."

"Well, you got more," she replied. The vaulted ceiling of the entry hall housed a gigantic copper and wood chandelier reminiscent of old Spain. Tile beneath her feet was done in a mosaic featuring rich reds and terra cottas that warmed the whole atmosphere.

Amy ran her hand appreciatively over the carving on the door. "This place is magnificent."

"I'm glad you like it," Mike said, smiling. "I don't have much company so I never got around to furnishing most of the rooms, but I suppose the place would be pretty stupendous if I gave it half a chance."

"Oh, yes," she said. And so would our relationship, she silently added.

Mike shut the door. He had assumed that the old, painful memories dogging him continually when he was at Amy's were the fault of her home and its welcoming aura. Now he wasn't so sure. As he watched her walk slowly down the long hall staring reverently at the house he'd never considered a real home, he began to see that his problem was less with their surroundings and more with Amy herself. It was she who had revived the longing in him for a place where he truly belonged. It was Amy, not her house, that was causing him such constant, painful turmoil.

"Did I win the contest?" she asked, jolting him from his reverie.

"I beg your pardon?"

"The photographs. Were mine judged the best?"

"It was a tie," Mike said. "I just felt that since I'd spent so much time camping on your doorstep, it was time I entertained you." And I mistakenly assumed I could escape feeling like an outsider at your house by bringing you here. Now I see that you belong wherever we are more than I do, he admitted cynically.

"That was nice of you."

"My pleasure."

"Could I see the photos? What I mean to say is, do you suppose I could have one of the ones I took of you?"

Mike shrugged. "Why?"

"Because I want one," she said as if explaining to a child. "I'm not going to throw darts at it, if that's what you're worried about."

"Sure. Wait here. I'll get you one."

Amy pivoted to watch him go. She'd bathed and perfumed every inch of herself, thinking as she performed the ritual that she was doing it to please Mike. Alone with him in the cavernous house, she began to question the purity of her motives. No matter what Marissa had said, it was wrong to think of trying to manipulate Mike by encouraging a physical contact he had said clearly he wanted to avoid.

Amy trembled inwardly, nervous about the direction her thoughts had taken lately. All she seemed able to concentrate on was Mike Dixon. All she cared about—really cared about—was his obvious quest for happiness. All she wanted was for him to love her.

Returning, he handed her an envelope containing seven snapshots. "These were all you took. I have no use for them, so you might as well have them."

"Thanks." Tucking them in her pocket, she followed as he led her past the formal dining room and into his kitchen. Bricks covered most of the walls, and dark red tile made up the floor. In the center of the room, opposite the sink, was an island containing a cooktop, a smaller sink and an overhead fan. Copper pots hung on one wall. From the look of them, they were seldom used.

"Oh, Mike." Amy walked quickly to the center island, her eyes wide. "This is wonderful. Think of all the fun we . . . I mean, you . . . could have in this kitchen!"

"I suppose." He smiled at her. "The thing it needs most, though, is a full-time maid. It took me hours to clean everything."

"You didn't have to do that for me," she said, smoothing her jeans and looking at her casual attire. "I dressed for a trip to the farm, as you can see."

"I noticed."

He went to one of the wide windows overlooking the barren land to the north and pointed. "Look. This is all that's left of somebody's lifelong dream. Apparently, the guy was no farmer and his jojoba bushes died before they could mature and begin to bear."

"That's sad," Amy said, joining him. "But at least he had the chance to try. Some people wish for things all their lives and never carry out their dreams even when they can." She folded her arms around herself. "My father was like that."

"What makes you think so?" Carefully nonchalant, Mike left her and began to assemble the food he'd bought especially for this evening along one side of the countertop.

Amy turned to watch him, leaning against the wide windowsill. "Oh, maybe because he talked a lot about settling down in one place but never did anything about it.

Until he had his stroke it seemed like his job kept him on the move all the time. When my mother died, I was sure he'd see what he'd missed and slow down a little, but the reverse was true.''

"He did research, you say?"

"That was his definition of the way he earned his living. Personally, I don't think he liked the job or the people he worked for very much."

"Oh?" Mike unwrapped a dish of potato salad he'd gotten at the deli. "Why?"

She shrugged. "I don't know. It was just a feeling I had." Crossing to him, she took the bowl and carried it to the small, square oak table he'd set in the corner of the kitchen near the widest windows. "I see why you didn't need the furniture I brought. What else can I do to help?"

"Nothing. I had a chicken barbecued for me and picked up the rest of dinner already prepared."

"If I hadn't eaten your stew I'd suspect you can't cook," Amy said pleasantly.

"I didn't get to town in time to do much except clean up this place," he confessed. "There was so much dust in here you could have raised jojobas on the windowsills!"

She laughed. "Good idea. Maybe they'd grow better inside."

"Maybe." Placing the chicken on the table, he gestured for her to join him.

"I'm glad you invited me here," Amy said, laying her napkin across her lap. "I was curious about your house."

"Why?"

"Oh, I don't know. Some people say a person's home tells a lot about them." And yours is transitory, Amy thought. You live as if it doesn't matter whether you ever come back here, almost as if you don't expect to return. There's little about the place that's distinctively yours. This house could belong to anyone. Or to no one.

"Let's not talk about houses," Mike suggested, eager to get to the reason he'd asked her to come. "Aren't you going to ask me how my business went?"

"No." Amy reached for the platter of chicken.

"Then I'll tell you anyway," he said. "But first I have to know if you're still interested in finding your birth parents."

Silence followed. Amy stared at him, her empty hand poised over the platter. "Is *that* where you were?"

Mike nodded.

"Why didn't you admit it when I asked you!"

"I wasn't certain I'd succeed."

Her fingers gripped the edge of the table. "And did you? Did you find them?"

"I think so." Pausing, he reached across for her hand. "The trouble is, we may never be able to prove it for sure."

"I don't care!" She clenched his hand. "Tell me everything. Don't tease me."

"Whoa," Mike said. "Let's eat while I fill you in."

"Oh, I couldn't. Not now." Leaning toward him Amy felt her eyes filling with tears. "Please?"

He rose and went to her, taking her hand to lead her down the hall. "Okay. Come into my office and we'll do this properly."

Mike had settled Amy in one of the smaller chairs while he took his place behind his desk. She'd begun to cry, as he knew she would, and he wanted to keep his distance rather than be tempted to take her in his arms to comfort her. If he once embraced her in earnest he doubted he'd have the willpower to let her go again.

"So my friend and I suspect that a nurse may have switched you for another woman's baby, then been forced to steal that child to cover the fact a switch had been made. Now that we've uncovered that much, my friend is looking for the nurse. However, if he doesn't locate her, or if she refuses to divulge what she knows, we may never be certain."

"I'm still not sure I follow it all," Amy said, sniffling. "Was I or wasn't I put up for adoption?"

This was where the situation got sticky, Mike thought. He'd have to be damn lucky to get away with the complicated lie he needed to tell to preserve Amy's tender memories of her father. Yes, she deserved to hear the truth, his conscience argued, but not if it destroyed her happiness. He knew what it was like to chase a false memory of a parent, and he wasn't going to contribute to Amy's disillusionment with hers.

"A young woman did enter Mercy Hospital to have a baby she intended to give to Martha and Ray Alexander." That much was true, Mike reminded himself to salve his conscience. "It's after the birth that the story gets clouded in supposition."

Amy leaned forward, raptly listening. "Go on."

"For whatever reasons, we think a nurse in the hospital switched your identification bracelet for that of another baby. There was so much confusion surrounding that infant's kidnapping, no one thought to check and see if the baby *remaining* in the nursery was the wrong one."

"How can you be so certain there was a switch made?"

"Two reasons. One, given some new evidence, the police now believe the nurse was lying about her complicity in the scheme."

"And the second?"

Opening a folder on his desk, Mike took out a photograph. "This is the second."

He turned the picture for her to see. It was of a happy bride and groom. The bride's wedding gown was dated, the photograph worn from its travels, but Amy saw immediately what had made Mike so adamantly certain he'd found her mother.

Amy stared at the picture. It was like looking into a mirror!

Chapter Twelve

Stunned by Mike's shocking revelations, Amy had asked for time alone, and he had granted her wish. Leaving her in his office, he made his way slowly back to the kitchen. Well, it was done. Amy now had enough of the facts concerning her origins to make up her mind whether to proceed or let the past stay buried. He hoped, for her sake, that she'd choose to forget about the confusing events shaping her destiny.

Would you? Mike asked himself. The scar on his cheek answered his question. No. He wouldn't be able to set aside his curiosity any more than he'd been able to stop himself from searching for his father.

He'd found him in a dirty bar at Third and Alvarado in downtown Los Angeles. The owner of Bennie's Pawn Shop, up the street, had told him where to look.

Mike had pushed open the door, and he remembered being greeted by the musty smell of stale smoke and too many unwashed bodies crowded into a small space. Inside, the wooden tables were ringed with countless wet-glass marks, and the floor was so neglected it was hard to tell what color it had once been. If a man at the bar hadn't identified himself, Mike would have passed him by, unrecognized.

"Dixon?" the man croaked, overhearing Mike's inquiry of the bartender. "Sure. Who wants him?"

Barely twenty years old, Mike had responded with more self-assurance than he felt. "I do. He's my father."

The man's laugh was derisive, his open mouth revealing discolored teeth, his unshaven face contorting in a cruel brand of humor. "You one of my bastards? Well, maybe." He took Mike's arm, trying to turn him around for a full view.

Mike shook loose. "I'm no bastard, and you know it! My mother was your wife. You ran out on us."

"Bull. I ain't never had a wife, at least not one I remember. If you're lookin' for a daddy, kid, you'd best keep on goin'."

Hardening his heart, Mike faced his father squarely. "You're him, all right. You might look different now, but I'll never forget that voice of yours. I remember how you yelled at my mother—how you'd come home drunk and take it out on her. She'd tell me to hide for my own protection, and when I did, I'd feel so damned guilty because I'd left her to face you alone."

"You always were a little coward, weren't you, boy?"

Mike felt ill. This animal was the father he'd spent months searching for. Well, he'd found him, and never again would he have to wonder if his memory had been distorted. His father was still every bit as evil as before.

A calloused hand shot out, catching Mike on the cheek before he could duck and knocking him against the bar. The old man had backhanded him across the face, his heavy ring making a half-moon-shaped slash over Mike's cheekbone.

Mike touched his fingers to the place where he'd been hit and felt the blood.

"That one's for your mama," the old man said.

"Yeah. Yeah, it sure is." Mike recalled pressing a hand-kerchief to his face. The injury couldn't make up for all the times his mother had protected him, but it had helped.

Scars are funny things, Mike marveled, stroking the small one on his cheek. Sometimes they go a lot deeper than your skin.

He put the potato salad in the refrigerator and settled down to wait for Amy.

By the time Amy joined him she'd made her decision. "I want you to contact the family you think is mine," she said. "If they're willing, I'd like to meet them."

"You're sure?" Damn, she looked stressed-out. With great effort, Mike subdued the urge to hold and comfort her.

"Yes and no. I think I'm more scared now that we're so close to answers than I was when we could only guess."

He nodded. "And if they refuse to meet with us?"

"Then I'll take that as a sign that I'm not supposed to press it."

"Fair enough."

Mike looked so worried about her Amy tried to smile for his sake. "You never told me their names," she said.

"Does it matter?" Opening the refrigerator, he got out the bowl of salad.

"No. Except that you sometimes make me feel like you don't fully trust me."

"That's not so," he countered.

"Then don't withhold parts of the story—please."

Could she actually read his mind? He walked to the table to replace the bowl and busied himself needlessly rearranging the silverware next to their places. He was tempted—Lord, he was tempted—but the facts behind his subterfuge stopped him. Amy didn't know what she was asking. The names of her birth parents were one thing, the real truth quite another. No good could possibly come of granting the substance of her request.

"Their name is Riggs," he said. "Now come and sit down. Our dinner is getting cold."

She smiled lovingly at him. "I wouldn't worry. It was cold when we started." Seating herself, she rested her folded hands in her lap. "Do they live in San Diego?"

"Who?"

"You know who. My parents."

Mike lifted his shoulders in a casual shrug. "I suppose so. The last address the police had for them was near Mission Bay. Chances are they're still there."

Helping herself to a roll, Amy concentrated on Mike. Something was wrong. He wasn't himself. Now that she thought about it, he hadn't seemed normal since she'd arrived.

"Mike?"

"Yes?" Reacting to the effects of the tension he was under, he knew he'd answered too abruptly. Amy's brow was creased, and she'd begun to regard him strangely.

"What's wrong?" she asked.

"Nothing."

Refolding her napkin, Amy placed it beside her plate and stood up. "Then why are you acting like Seymour does when he knows he's misbehaved and is waiting for me to discover what he's done?"

Mike raised his hands in mock surrender. "You've caught me. I confess."

"Mike . . . Stop teasing."

He reached up, took her hand and urged her to sit down again. "Amy, take it easy. You're nervous and upset because it's time for you to make some serious decisions. That's natural, believe me."

His thumb caressed the back of her hand. "Lots of silly things are going to bother you at a time like this. I know that. If I seem to be taking your struggles lightly, it's only because the situation is so common to me."

Lightly? she mused. That was hardly the description she'd have given Mike's attitude. However, he was right about one thing—she was new to all this, and he wasn't. Whatever his reasons, she supposed it was irrational to expect him to view her dilemma as dramatically as she did.

"I'm sorry," Amy finally said, trying to muster a genuine smile. "I honestly thought I wanted to know everything. I guess I was fooling myself into believing it wouldn't be traumatic when it finally happened."

"Nothing has actually happened yet," Mike reminded her. "But you must understand that once we contact Mr. and Mrs. Riggs there will be no going back."

"I know," Amy said quietly. "If you're correct about the switching of the two babies and subsequent kidnapping of one, they're as much a victim as the baby was—as I am— and they have as much right to the truth."

She managed a smile. "It's a lot like being two separate people. I can stand back and be Amy Alexander while I consider the stolen baby and imagine her as someone apart from myself."

Chuckling, she shook her head. "Oh, dear! Don't repeat what I just said, or they're liable to come to get me with butterfly nets and a straitjacket."

"Don't worry, honey," Mike said. "You've just received a pretty bad shock. These things take some getting used to."

"Did you ever get used to whatever it was that made you such an unhappy child?" she asked cautiously, her eyes bathing him in empathetic kindness.

"Humpf. No." Mike released her hand and stared at his plate for a few seconds. Then he raised his eyes to meet Amy's. "Besides, it wasn't any one thing, if that's what you mean. Losing my mother was just a tiny part."

"Do you ever talk about the rest of it?" Amy purposely kept her voice soft, her tone gentle.

Mike's penetrating stare seemed to delve into her soul. Hardened and stoic, his expression left no room for discussion. "No," he said. "I never do."

Mike had stared out the window of the 727 and thought about Amy all the way to San Diego. He purposely hadn't touched her again or kissed her goodbye when she'd left his house. The pain and need in her expression had affected him, yes, but it seemed as if he was finally immune to the emotions that had manipulated his actions in the past.

Amy was about to regain a portion of the family she had lost. He'd see to that. And as for himself and his own needs? They didn't matter, he argued. They never had. Not really. Thinking of a future with Amy had been a foolish fantasy he'd stupidly allowed himself to consider. In a few days or weeks she'd no longer need him, and his part in her life would be over. It was as simple as that.

Parking his rented Ford at the curb in front of the Riggs' house, he straightened his tie, slipped his suit jacket on and fastened one button. He had to look businesslike as well as trustworthy.

Always a little nervous in similar instances, he now found he had sweaty palms and a mouth so dry he couldn't comfortably swallow. This encounter was the most important in his career. This was for Amy.

Standing in front of the brown and white stucco house, he double-checked the two-year-old address Finch had given him, squared his shoulders and started up the brick-lined front walk. No name on the mailbox confirmed that the house's occupants were the same as when Finch had last talked to them, but he had to start somewhere. Mike rang the bell.

The young man who opened the door was fair, almost red-haired, and nearly as tall as Mike. Barefoot, he was dressed in blue nylon boxer shorts and a cut-off sweatshirt and eating an apple.

"Yes?"

"I'd like to see John or Susan Riggs, please," Mike said.

"What for?"

Mike presented his card. "I have some information for them. May I come in?"

The athletic young man eyed the card. "What's this all about?"

"Please." Courteously, Mike gestured through the open door. "It's best discussed in private."

Smaller and gently spoken, a woman in her forties appeared behind the young man in the doorway. "What is it, Shane?"

He passed the card to her. "This guy wants to see you, Mom. He won't say why, and he can't know us because he asked for Dad, too."

Sad, gray eyes studied first the card, then Mike, before the woman spoke. "My husband passed away last year. Unless you have news of my daughter, we have nothing to discuss."

Reaching into his pocket, Mike produced the photograph he'd taken of Amy. As he passed it to Mrs. Riggs, he said, "You be the judge."

She blinked rapidly as tears filled her eyes. In seconds Shane had stepped between his mother and Mike. "Get out of here, mister. We don't need your kind coming around and stirring things up. You hear?"

Mike stood his ground, watching Susan Riggs. It was up to her to decide. If she rejected the idea that Amy might be her daughter, there was nothing more he could do. If not, he'd face off with the boy.

"It could be," she muttered before laying her hand on Shane's arm to restrain him. "Let him come in."

"But..." Reluctantly, Shane stepped aside.

"Thank you," Mike said, following her into the modest living room. "I appreciate the chance to acquaint you with my client."

Shane pitched the remains of his apple out the door and followed Mike, his fists clenched. "You can tell your client that we have no money," he said icily. "Mom's a widow, and she and Dad spent so much looking for my lost sister we have very little left to spare now. Whoever your client is, she won't get a damn dime out of us."

Mike addressed Mrs. Riggs, ignoring Shane. "As you can see from the house in the photograph, Amy is comfortably well-off. You have nothing to fear from her."

"Go on, Mr..." she referred to Mike's business card, "Dixon." Perching on the edge of a straight chair, she gestured for Mike to sit on the couch. When he did, Shane hovered next to him.

"We have reason to believe my client, Ms. Alexander, may be the daughter who was taken from you twenty-three years ago."

Susan smiled sadly. "Forgive me and my son for doubting you, Mr. Dixon, but we've been through so much in the past with no results whatsoever, we tend to be skeptical."

"I understand," Mike told her, also nodding to Shane. "At first, I advised my client to forget the whole affair and get on with her life. As you can see from my presence here, she refused to be deterred."

"*That's* a Riggs trait," Susan said, smiling more broadly at her son. She gazed at the photograph she still held. "And there is a family resemblance."

Probably less now than there once was, Mike thought. The years of searching for her lost baby had taken a visible toll on Susan Riggs.

"We thought so," he said. "The police are also interested again, even though one or more of the original perpetrators of the crime are deceased."

Shane began to curse, and his mother shushed him with a simple gesture. "Come here and tell me what you think," she said, holding up the snapshot.

"Ah, who cares what I think," he said. "If you need me to throw this guy out, I'll be in my room."

"He's not had an easy life," Susan explained as Shane left them. "I'm afraid the loss of my first baby made me an overprotective mother. Shane grew up in the shadow of a sister he never knew. While we concentrated on searching for her, he was neglected sometimes."

"I do understand," Mike said. "It might please you to know that Amy had a loving, caring home in which to mature."

"Is that her name? We called our baby Christina, after my mother, but Amy seems to suit the girl I see in this picture."

"She's a lovely person. I've never been one to try to second-guess the facts, but I'd say you and she are quite a bit alike."

"Is that so?" Mrs. Riggs's eyes filled with more moisture. "Then start from the beginning and tell me the whole story, Mr. Dixon. I want to hear everything you know about this pretty girl."

"Before I begin, there's one favor I need to ask."

"Yes?" Susan's hands cupped the cherished photograph.

"Some of the facts of the case point to criminal activity on the part of one of the parents who loved and raised Amy. I want to ask your promise you won't divulge that information to her if I tell you what I suspect."

"You'd trust me to do that?" Susan's eyes widened exactly the way Mike had seen Amy express similar astonishment.

"I have to," he confessed. "Without all the facts you won't understand what happened and why it's so important that you agree to at least one meeting with Amy."

"All right," Susan said. "I promise. Whatever you choose to tell me won't go any farther than this room."

"Agreed."

Mike leaned forward, rested his elbows on his knees and began to speak. "It all started when Amy came to me several months ago with the story that she'd been adopted."

Thankful she was in her office when Mike's call came, Amy sank into her desk chair while she listened to him relate the details of his meeting with her birth mother.

"And she's agreed to see me?" Amy asked breathlessly, clutching the receiver. "Oh, Mike. That's wonderful! When?"

He leaned back on the king-size bed in his hotel room and stared blankly at the mirror over the blond oak dressing table. "This weekend. I'm still in San Diego. Would you be willing to come down here to see her?"

"Of course! You know I would." Amy's voice quieted. "Is she nice? I realize that's an awful thing to ask but I'm absolutely *terrified* of meeting her."

He laughed, stretching out on the rose-patterned bedspread. "She's quite a lot like you, actually."

"Uh-oh. Is that good or bad?"

"It's good, honey. Don't worry. She'll love you."

"Do you really think so?" Amy paused. "Mike? Are you sure she's the one?"

"I'm positive now," he said. Finch had located the long-lost nurse Billingsly, and in return for a promise of immunity she had confessed to her part in the crime.

Billingsly's complicity was one of the crucial details he had imparted to Susan Riggs. The other was the nurse's story of her original recruitment by Ray Alexander and their theft of the substituted Riggs baby to cover the switch of the infants. That it had been a foolproof plan was witnessed by the fact that no one would have suspected the truth if Martha Alexander, in her innocence, hadn't left a smattering of clues.

"Then you set it up," Amy told him. "Whatever she wants to do and wherever she wants to meet is fine with me. I'll be there."

"Amy?" Mike's voice was low, and he spoke tentatively. "Yes?"

"Don't get your hopes up too much. Sometimes meetings like these work out well and sometimes they don't."

"I know." What was he withholding? she wondered. "Talk to me, Mike. Why did you warn me like that?"

"There's another member of the family besides your mother, a nineteen-year-old son, Shane."

"I have a brother? Oh, Mike, how wonderful!"

"Shane doesn't think so," Mike said. "In fact, I've suggested that your first meeting with Susan Riggs be arranged to exclude him."

Quietly thoughtful, Amy considered the piece of information Mike had just imparted. "Why do you think he's hostile?"

"Best guess? He felt left out, as a child, with so much emphasis being placed on his missing sister. Later, when his father died, he took his place as Susan's protector."

Mike paused. "Shane is afraid of you, Amy. He doesn't want his mother hurt and he doesn't want to lose the special place he's made for himself in her life."

"Then invite him," Amy ordered. "He belongs there when my mother and I meet for the first time."

"Are you sure?"

"Yes. And you come, too. I want all the special people in my life around me when I take the big step."

"All right," Mike promised, glad he'd have a plausible excuse to be on hand to look out for Amy's interests, especially since she'd chosen to include Shane. "Can you get away this weekend?"

"I'll manage. Marissa can handle Marino's for me, and I'll ask Mrs. Norton to pop in and feed Seymour."

"Good. Catch a commuter flight from Palm Springs to San Diego, and I'll meet you at the airport. I don't want you trying to drive all that way with so much on your mind."

"How can I reach you to let you know the time?" Amy was fumbling around looking for a pencil.

"I'm staying at the Hilton downtown," he said. "Room 606."

"Room 606. Got it." She blinked to clear her vision. "Mike?"

"Yes?"

"Thank you," she said emotionally. "For everything."

"Maybe you'd better wait till you meet your mother before you thank me."

Good old Mike—always cautious. Amy smiled into the receiver. "Nope. However this turns out, I'll never forget that you've done your best for me."

You'll forget, Mike thought. Instead of voicing his conclusion he said, "Then you're quite welcome, Ms. Alexander. Now, get on the phone to the airlines and book your flight."

"Yes, sir." Amy was grinning through a veil of happy tears. "I'll call you back as soon as I know when I'm arriving."

Chapter Thirteen

Amy raised her seat back to the fully upright position to comply with the flight attendant's request. The flashing message on the ceiling above her advised that all seat belts be fastened prior to the plane's imminent arrival in San Diego.

Fussing with her sleeveless blue voile dress, Amy adjusted the short, boxy, linen jacket over it for the hundredth time. She knew Mike would like the outfit, but was it appropriate for the rest of her planned encounter? What *did* one wear to the first meeting with one's mother, anyway?

Picturing an infant in gown, bonnet and booties, she started to giggle. Getting off the plane dressed like that would be a picture, wouldn't it? Babies certainly had it easier than adults. They had no choice of what to wear so they were always acceptably clad!

Laughing nervously, Amy saw the approaching runway as a gray blur out the plane's window, and thoughts of Mike superseded all others. He'd be there waiting, and she could rush into his arms and tap his strength to pull herself together before her meeting with Mrs. Riggs.

Mrs. Riggs. Susan, Mike had said. What should she call her? How should she address the woman who might have been so familiar, yet wasn't? Amy picked up her white shoulder bag, set it on her lap and hugged it to her.

The wheels touched ground, and she took a deep breath. The plane turned and began to taxi toward the terminal. And what about Shane? Whatever his attitude was, Amy vowed she would greet him politely and show by her actions that she posed no threat to either his place in the family or his mother's love. A piece of cake, as Marissa would say.

Amy had purposely traveled light, bringing only a small, carry-on bag in addition to her purse. Mike had promised to arrange a room for her at the Hilton near his, and she couldn't help being excited about the prospect of that, as well.

All in all, she decided, unfastening her seat belt and retrieving her blue nylon bag from the overhead compartment, this promised to be one *very* extraordinary weekend.

Caught in the crush of the deplaning passengers, Amy inched her way toward the door.

"Have a nice day," a stewardess said.

Amy's grin was broad. "Oh, I plan on it!"

Once out onto the covered walkway she was able to circumvent some of the slower-moving people and hurry toward the gate. She saw Mike the minute she turned the corner into the main concourse, and her heart began to pound relentlessly.

As promised, he was standing just past the end of the tunnel leading from gate fifty-four. His light brown suit was neatly pressed, his hair perfectly combed, and except for the absence of the welcoming smile she had expected to see on his face, he looked better than ever.

Amy shouldered her way through the crowd. "Mike!" Running the last few yards she dropped her bag at his feet and flew into his arms.

"Oh, Mike! I'm so glad to see you."

He caught her up in his embrace, held her tightly for a moment, then reached to grasp her arms. Releasing her grip on his neck, he placed her at arm's length. "Was it a bad flight?"

"No. It just seemed to take forever, that's all. I missed you so! I could hardly wait to get here and give you the big hug you deserve." She studied his subdued expression. "Is everything okay? You look funny."

"Everything's fine," he said evenly. "I'm to take you straight to the meeting. Your mother is as excited about it as you are."

"Now? Oh, dear!" She peered over his shoulder at her reflection on the window of the gift and souvenir shop and smoothed her hair. "Don't I get a chance to freshen up first?" She spun in a circle in front of him. "Isn't this a gorgeous dress?"

"Yes. You look fine, Amy. You're not trying out for a part in a movie, you know. This is just your mother you're meeting."

"And my brother. You did invite Shane, didn't you?" Amy slipped her hand through the crook of Mike's arm as he hefted her bag and started down the wide, carpeted hallway toward the outer terminal.

"I invited him."

"And he came?" She was looking up at Mike, still unsure as to what emotions she was seeing in his gravely stoic expression.

"He came."

Amy saw Mike's jaw muscles tighten, and she laid her free hand on his upper arm with a friendly pat. "It'll be all right. You'll see."

"Yes, I guess I will."

He'd slowed his pace, and Amy urged him ahead. "Come on."

Taking her hand from his arm, Mike pulled her back. "No. Wait."

She searched his eyes. They were an intense, rich brown, and his gaze was so solemn she did exactly as he ordered, staring at him. "What is it, Mike? What's wrong?"

His expression softened. Gently he grasped her shoulders, turning her away from him. "Nothing's wrong. Look."

The passing crowd parted for Amy as if they'd rehearsed the scene. There, standing against the red-carpeted wall, was a frail, nervous-looking woman in a rose-colored dress. Next to her stood a young man with both hands stuffed in his pockets and a dour countenance.

The woman was looking at Amy with a tenderness born of expectation and love. There were tears in her eyes.

Amy shot a questioning glance at Mike and he nodded. "That's her? And Shane?"

"Yes." Giving her a little push, Mike hung back while Amy took the longest ten-yard walk of her life.

Across the void, Susan took one tentative step, then another. Clutching her white handbag by its thin strap, she started to smile.

In seconds, Amy stood facing her birth mother. She put out her trembling hand. When Susan grasped it, hers, too, was shaking. Simultaneously, they glanced at their quaking fingers and burst into quiet giggles.

"Hello," Amy said. "I see we have one thing in common already."

"Yes. So it seems." Sniffling, Susan slid the strap of her purse over her forearm and covered Amy's hand with hers. "This is scary, isn't it?"

Amy nodded. "Very. You don't know how many times I went over what I was going to say to you. Now, I can't remember one lucid sentence!"

"Oh, yes, I do know," Susan confessed, grinning. Her eyes were clouded with moisture. "I've been talking to myself for three days."

Seeing the tears welling in her mother's eyes, Amy felt her own filling to the brim. In seconds, they spilled out to roll down her cheeks. Unashamed, she let them flow unhindered.

Susan was the first to move. Opening her arms to the daughter she'd thought she would never know, she welcomed Amy.

As naturally as if they'd always been close, Amy returned her mother's display of affection and they stood, silently weeping and clinging to each other until a strange male voice disturbed the beauty of the moment.

"Very touching. What comes next?"

Susan straightened, wiping her eyes. She kept one arm around Amy and reached out with her other. "I'm sorry. I should have introduced you two right away."

She took her son's hand in hers. "Shane, this is your sister. Amy, this is Shane."

Amy smiled through her tears as she extended her hand to her brother. "How do you do?"

"Not as well as I used to before your friend showed up," Shane said. Refusing to shake Amy's hand, he cocked his head toward Mike.

Amy felt Susan stiffen and put up her hand to stop the woman from rebuking Shane.

"It's all right," Amy said. "These things take time."

"Time?" Shane snorted derisively. "How much time have you got, lady? Enough to make up for my father's early death and all the suffering your 'family' caused mine?"

"Shane!" Susan put both hands on his arm. "Stop this!"

He shook her off. "Stop what, Mother? Stop telling the truth?" He rolled his eyes toward the ceiling and shouted, "My God, Mom! She was raised by a man who was a damn kidnapper, and you welcome her like she was one of us?

How pure and innocent do you think she can be? Don't we owe Dad *anything*?''

Speechless, Amy could only stare at Susan's anguished face. If her expression was to be trusted, what Shane had claimed was true! Only it couldn't be. It just couldn't be! Her father would never...

Amy was standing perfectly still, her eyes as wide as a frightened doe's, when Mike grabbed Shane by the left shoulder and spun him around.

Mike's glaring anger was reflected in the glance he shot at Susan Riggs. "Why?" he demanded.

"He's my son. He deserved to know."

"And you thought, in his state of mind, that he'd actually keep that information to himself?"

Susan's gaze lowered to the floor. "Yes. I thought he would."

"Well, you were wrong." Mike turned his attention to Amy. "I'm sorry. I tried to keep it from you."

"No! It can't be."

He reached for Amy's arm. "I wish it weren't so."

"But..." Incredulous, she stared at him. If there was anything she had learned in her short association with Mike Dixon, it was to read the truth when it appeared in his eyes. Yet she still struggled to believe him. "Dad wouldn't do something like that. It can't be true."

Shane stood clear of Mike. "Oh, it's true, all right, and I don't for one minute believe you didn't know it, Ms. Alexander." He voiced her name as if it were an anathema.

Mike's clenched fist rose in Amy's defense, but she grabbed his arm before he could act and swung around to stand between Mike's fury and the outspoken brother she'd just met.

Susan gasped, grasping Mike's jacket and trying to restrain him, as well.

"Stop it!" Amy ordered. "All of you. Just stop it." They'd drawn a crowd that included airport security guards, and she certainly didn't want Mike or Shane arrested.

Susan reached out to her. "I am sorry. I didn't mean for this to happen."

"But it has," Amy said sadly. She pushed Mike's arms to his sides, finding little resistance, and looked at him. "So this is what you've been hiding all along."

The disappointment he read in her eyes was overshadowed only by his own sense of failure. He should never have trusted Susan Riggs. The trouble was, she'd reminded him so strongly of Amy he'd gotten careless. Now he *and* Amy were paying for his stupidity.

What alternative did he have except to confess? "I wasn't certain until three days ago."

"But you suspected before that?"

Mike nodded. "Yes."

"Oh, yeah," Shane piped up from behind her. "Make it good, both of you."

Amy spun around to face him. "Oh, stop it! I care what you think of me, Shane, but I care even more about our mother. You're hurting her, and I'll thank you to keep your rotten attitudes to yourself."

His jaw slackened as she went on, "And in case it matters, no, I *didn't* know about my father—my adoptive father—and even if I had, that doesn't change the fact that he and Mom loved me, and in spite of everything, I still love them."

Trembling with anger and emotion, she nevertheless held her head high. "You might keep in mind how much your mother loves you and consider her feelings a little more in the future."

Amy turned to Mike and Susan. "As for me, I need some time alone, if you don't mind."

"I'll take you to the hotel," Mike said.

"No." She picked up her bag. "I'd rather get there by myself."

"Will we see you later?" Susan asked, her voice near breaking.

"If you still want to, it can be arranged," Amy said quietly. "Mike knows where I'll be."

It was hard to maintain her dignity, to refrain from letting loose the scream of release that hovered so close to the surface. This was all so unfair! Her pretty dreams had become a nightmare.

Her spine stiff, Amy turned and walked toward the doors leading into the bright San Diego sunshine. She could feel all their eyes on her, but she never wavered, never once looked back.

"I ought to..." Mike glared at Shane. "Oh, what the hell. It's too late to change anything."

The young man's shoulders slumped. "She's for real, isn't she?"

"You're just now discovering that?" Mike snapped. "Terrific!"

Dabbing at her eyes, Susan spoke up. "She'll be all right. She's had a bad shock, but she's my daughter. She'll survive."

"Plain survival isn't exactly what I had in mind for Amy," Mike said. "People like her don't deserve to have bad things happen to them. She's too nice, too sweet and honest."

"You mustn't blame yourself. What happened was my fault, and Shane's, and you have my deepest apology." Susan touched his arm. "I know you care for her. That will help her recover, too."

"She's just a client," Mike insisted.

Susan smiled at him. "She's just a client the same way an eight-point earthquake is just a little shake, Mr. Dixon."

She took his arm and her son's hand. "Come on, you two. Let's follow her to the hotel. I don't think it will be too long before Amy is ready to talk to us."

Shane looked at her questioningly. "How can you be sure? She'll probably *never* speak to me again."

"Oh, she will," Susan said. "And she won't hold a grudge against Mr. Dixon, here, either. She's far too decent for that."

"You *do* like her, don't you?" Mike observed.

"I think she's wonderful." Susan looked at him with love glowing in her eyes. "And so are the both of you, in spite of all your faults."

"Would you call me Mike?"

"I'd love to. And you call me Susan." She grinned with mischief in her expression. "Shane you already know by his first name. Him, you may call *anything you like*, at least until our Amy has bounced back and I'm through being mad at him."

Amy caught the airport limousine to the Hilton. Tall and imposing, the hotel stood overlooking the low Pacific coastline. In the bay, small sailboats vied with tankers for their share of the blue-green ocean, and seabirds soared and darted over the water.

The uniformed limo driver pulled up under the covered entryway, got out and reached to help her with her bag. "I see you don't travel with a lot of excess baggage."

His remark struck her funny in spite of, or perhaps because of, the extraordinary morning she'd had. "Not with suitcases, if that's what you mean," she said wryly. "It seems, however, that I have been dealing with a different kind of excess baggage all my life."

He laughed. "Sounds like all the rest of us, lady."

Amy tipped him and nodded as a hotel bellman picked up her tiny bag. "Not quite. Mine is a *lot* heavier than most."

The lobby was impressive with its rich marble floors, tall Grecian columns and elegantly understated decor. A friendly desk clerk in a wine-colored blazer quickly programmed Amy's name and credit-card number into the hotel's computer and handed her a pass to her room.

"You're in 604, Ms. Alexander. This is our new computer key system. Just insert this card in the slot in your door and turn the knob when the green light begins to blink."

"Thank you."

"Please call if we can be of any service," the clerk said.

Amy wondered absently if the hotel had a professional friend on staff. She could certainly use one.

Nodding pleasantly, she turned and started up in the elevator, accompanied by the bellman and her ridiculously small bag. She'd briefly considered telling him she could manage it herself, then changed her mind. He was like her staff at Marino's—a man doing his job. It wouldn't be fair to deprive him of the chance to earn a few more dollars.

She tipped him at her door and entered the room alone, glad to have finally found sanctuary and solitude. Slipping her shoes off, she padded across the thick carpet to the window and drew open the heavy brocade drapes.

Standing by the window, Amy gazed at the breathtaking view. There was a certain freedom inherent in the vast expanse of the ocean, and seeing it all from above made it feel even greater.

She sighed. So, her father *had* been involved in shameful activities. Well, at least now that it had been confirmed she could stop berating herself for suspecting as much.

It was his bosses who had dragged him down, she was certain. And once he was involved she supposed there was no going back. Poor man! That was undoubtedly why he'd refused to talk about his work. How alone he must have felt, unable to confide in either his wife or daughter.

Amy rested one hand on the edge of the drape and shook her head as she considered her mother's and father's relationship. She was certain there was no chance Martha had known or even suspected Ray was involved in anything criminal. She was too naive.

And Amy herself? Well, she reasoned, a young girl wasn't expected to be cognizant of her father's business dealings, at least not when he went to such great lengths to keep them from her. No. She deserved none of Ray's guilt, even by association.

Yet there had been terrible damage done to the Riggs family. Whatever the details of the crime, they had been hurt beyond comprehension, and there had to be some way Amy could make up for at least a small portion of their anguish. She'd have to try.

A door slamming in the distance caught her attention and she stood very still, listening intently. From what she could hear through the thick walls, Mike had returned to his room. Her heart skipped a beat and began to speed. She wasn't ready to face him. Not yet. But she did want to hear the rest of the story about Ray and the Riggs kidnapping.

Leaving the window, she walked to the telephone beside the bed, lifted the receiver and dialed Mike's room.

"Hello."

"Mike? It's Amy."

"I know." He waited for her to go on.

"I want you to tell me everything you've found out about my father."

His gut tied in a hard knot. "What good will that do? He's dead. Let the truth die, too."

"It doesn't work that way for me, Mike," she explained softly. "My future will always be clouded if I don't know it all."

Her future. Mike sank to the edge of his bed. "All right. Do you want to meet me somewhere?" He held his breath, praying she wouldn't ask him to come to her room. He didn't want to love her and leave her, and he was afraid he'd be pushing his already shaky self-control over its limits if he allowed himself to be alone with her again.

"No," she said. "Tell me now. Like this."

Releasing the pent-up air from his lungs, Mike agreed. "Okay. If you're standing up you'd better sit down. Do you want it all? Every detail?"

"Yes. Imagining what might have motivated my father is far worse than facing the truth," she said wisely. "Tell me everything."

"All right." Mike took a deep breath and began. "Your father arranged to have a baby born at Mercy Hospital to a woman using your mother's name—probably a lot like the surrogates of today only without anyone else's knowledge. She was the natural mother, but using Martha's name would have eliminated the need for adoption and given him clear claim to that child, but something evidently went wrong."

"What?"

"We don't know for sure. We suspect, from information given to the police by a nurse, that there was something wrong with that particular baby. Anyway, a switch was made, the Alexander baby for the Riggs baby. That's you. The woman masquerading as Martha was discharged to take you home, and the other baby, by then identified as Christina Riggs, had to be stolen to cover the switch.''

"Okay," Amy said slowly. "That explains about those two infants, but what about the rest of the babies? According to the newspaper, two others also disappeared from the hospital at about the same time.''

Mike's voice was low, sad. "Those babies found their way into the black market. As far as we can tell, they were taken only to camouflage Ray's elaborate plan to gain you as his own daughter.''

"So I was never actually adopted at all!''

"No. And the baby who was initially supposed to go to Ray and Martha was sold to the highest bidder.''

Amy was overwhelmed by the gravity of her father's misdeeds. "Oh, Mike. How dreadful!''

"Can you see why I tried to keep this from you?''

"Yes." As she stared out the window at the clear sky, it was hard for her to imagine that Ray had really done all that Mike claimed. "And my mother?" Amy asked. "Did she know?''

"She couldn't have," Mike explained tenderly. "Ray's scheme had to include deceiving her. She evidently thought they'd adopted you legally. He must have insisted they keep the facts from you until you were an adult, but she was too sentimental about your origins not to keep a sketchy record.''

"The scrapbook.''

"Yes. She must have included the clippings about the missing babies as a way of reminding herself how lucky she was to have you, safe and well.''

"Is that all?''

"Isn't it enough?''

"Yes," Amy said slowly, softly. "I guess it is."

"Susan and Shane are waiting downstairs in the lounge," he said. "They'd like to talk to you."

Amy sighed. "I owe them a great deal, don't I, Mike?"

"You can't be held responsible for someone else's crimes," he insisted. "It's none of your business what Ray did to get you. Not really."

"He was my father," Amy said sadly. "Whatever he did, he was still my father and always will be. Whether he was an honest man or not, that makes it my business."

"I guess so," Mike conceded. "All right. What do you want me to tell Susan? Shall I send her home?"

"No." Straightening, Amy glanced at her reflection in the vanity mirror. "Give me a few minutes to pull myself together and I'll meet you all downstairs in the lounge."

"You're sure this is what you want to do?"

"If I run from it, it will be much harder. It's what I have to do," Amy said. "Right now, I can't think beyond that."

Chapter Fourteen

Amy locked the door behind her and started down the brightly carpeted hall to the elevator. In retrospect, it was quite obvious why Mike had lied. Not that he was right to do it, she added to herself quickly, but his motives had been noble even if his actions had fallen short. He'd been protecting her. She could hardly hold that against him. And he'd have gotten away with his subterfuge, too, if Shane hadn't been so hotheaded and jealous.

The doors opened and Amy stepped aboard, glad there was no one else in the elevator to disturb her thoughts. Poor Shane. And poor Mike. He'd gone to a lot of trouble to try to shield her memory of her father. Thinking back on both her childhood and Mike's recent actions, the whole puzzle made a lot more sense than it once had.

She pushed the button for the lobby. It wasn't that hard to imagine Ray's double life. Secretive and vague, he'd undoubtedly fooled her mother just as he'd fooled everyone else. For Amy the worst part of the whole story was that she could never give back the years her father had stolen from the Riggs family.

But we can all start over today, she countered. Determined to succeed, she stood straighter, smiled and stepped into the lobby. Her heels clicked on the marble floor as she made her way to the sunken area that served as the hotel's piano bar and lounge. Seated on one of the striped sofas was a red-eyed Susan Riggs. Shane held her hand.

It was Mike who rose to greet Amy. She could see from his hesitancy that he was still unsure how well she'd accepted the truth, and she made up her mind to set him at ease.

"Hello, Mike," Amy said brightly, reaching for his hand. "I'm sorry if I kept you waiting."

He led her to the settee opposite Susan and Shane and seated her. "Can I get you a drink?"

"No, thank you." She patted the cushion next to her and paused until Mike joined her. "I don't need alcohol to help me cope with my checkered past." Taking Mike's hand for moral support, Amy smiled at him as he put his other arm around her.

She turned to her brother. "I'm glad you came to the hotel. It saves me a trip looking for you, and I can say what needs to be said without wasting time."

"There's nothing for you to say, dear," Susan interjected. "Shane is too big to spank, but I assure you, we're both sorry to have caused you the distress of hearing about your father so bluntly."

"It's all right." Amy meant it. "Just try not to blame me for the terrible things he did."

Susan reached out to her. "We don't, Amy." Susan cast a sidelong glance at her son. "*Neither* of us do."

Coloring, Shane merely nodded agreement, and Amy redirected the conversation to spare him the necessity of a verbal affirmation. His concurrence was enough.

"Then I think we should all take time out, get to know each other and unwind," Amy suggested. "How about later this afternoon? We could meet at the harbor and watch the sea gulls, or do whatever you San Diego natives recommend.''

''I have a good idea,'' Susan said. ''Our place is near the beach on Mission Bay. You and Shane could even walk down to the ocean and look for shells.''

Amy's smile was growing. ''If he promises not to try to drown me,'' she said, half-teasing the teenager.

Blushing, Shane glanced at Mike's arm resting protectively on Amy's shoulders. ''Not a chance. Not with your bodyguard on duty. He looks like he'd murder me if I so much as splashed you!''

Mike confirmed the younger man's conclusions. ''You're darned right.'' His eyes narrowed. ''And even when I'm not here, I'll expect you to treat your sister with respect. Understood?''

Shane averted his eyes. ''Understood.''

''Good.''

Smiling, Amy got to her feet and grasped Susan's hands tightly. ''Then it's settled. Mike knows how to get to your house, doesn't he? What time would you like us to come?''

''Two or three o'clock is fine.'' She was beaming happily. ''The sooner the better. We have a lot of catching up to do. And please, dress casually. We're not fancy people.''

Amy laughed. ''Neither am I. Can I bring anything? Food? Beverages?''

''No, no. We'll plan a barbecue, won't we, Shane?'' Susan squeezed her daughter's hand as they started for the door together. ''The most important thing is that you'll be there.''

''We will be. It's a promise,'' Amy said. Casting a side-long glance at Mike, she expected to see his familiar grin and arched eyebrow. Instead, he was following along behind, viewing the scene expressionlessly.

''Won't we, Mike?'' Amy urged.

''Of course. Now, if you'll all excuse me . . .''

Amy watched him walk to the elevator and get in. Puzzled, she turned to Susan. "That's funny. I thought he'd be so happy for me—for us."

"He cares for you a great deal," Susan volunteered.

"I hope so." Her confession caused Amy to blush.

"He does. It shows in the way he looks at you when you don't know he's doing it. He's a quiet man, but oftentimes those are the best kind. Their emotions run deep."

Susan laughed lightly and finished wiping the tear streaks from her cheeks. "Listen to me, will you? I sound like..." She stopped herself.

Amy finished the sentence for her. "You sound like my mother, and that's just fine with me."

"This will take some getting used to, won't it?" Susan asked.

Laughing with her, Amy agreed. "But we'll adjust." She held out her hand to Shane. "Truce?"

He took it gladly. "Yeah. Sorry."

"Forget it. You were just protecting someone you love. Which reminds me..." Amy's eyes strayed to the elevators. "If you'll excuse me, I think I'll go see if Mother knows best."

"About Mr. Dixon?"

"About strong, quiet men and love," Amy said. "I sure hope she's right."

Susan patted Amy's hand. "Good luck, dear."

"Thanks." Amy pressed her lips tightly together, then convinced herself a smile was better. "I'm afraid I'll need all the luck I can get."

When Amy first knocked on Mike's door and got no answer, she began to wonder if he'd failed to return to his room. Determined to be certain before giving up, she banged louder.

"Mike? Are you in there?"

Silence. Amy looked left and right, saw no witnesses and chanced a bit of innocent pandemonium. "All right, Mike Dixon. You asked for it."

Clutching her hands beneath her chin for effect, she began to wail loudly, "You shouldn't have deserted me and our twelve kids like you did, Michael. The rent's past due and after the pictures they took of the armored car robbery I can't show my face on the streets anymore." Her voice rose another decibel. "It's pitiful! Just pitiful!"

Mike jerked open the door, grabbed her by the arm and hustled her inside. A scowl shrouded his face. "What was *that* all about?"

"I got in, didn't I?" Amy looked past him to the bed. His suitcase lay open. It was nearly filled. "Are you going somewhere?"

"Home. My business here is finished."

"Your business? Is that all I am to you?"

"What I do or don't feel about you is unimportant, Amy." He returned to his packing, flinging a shirt and tie into the top of the bag in a jumbled pile.

"Unimportant to you?"

"Unimportant, period."

"And just what gave you that idea?" Amy demanded. "Don't *I* have any say in the matter?"

"Say whatever you want to. It won't change the facts." He zipped the top of his shaving kit, tucked it in beside the shirt and closed the bag.

"Which are?" Amy refused to let him walk out of her life without explaining. She didn't know what she could do or say to make him see that they belonged together but she reasoned she was better off trying than giving up without a fight.

"You have what you wanted, Amy," he said flatly. "You have a family again. I'll leave you the rental car and directions to the Riggs house. Susan likes you, and I'm sure your charms will win Shane over in no time. That's all there is to tell.''

"Oh, it is, is it?" Standing with her hands on her hips she blocked Mike's exit. "And what about us—you and me?"

"There is no *us*, Amy."

"I don't believe you." Her limbs were trembling, yet she stood firmly in his way.

"What you need is time to calm down and think this through," Mike said. He started to shoulder past her. "In a few days you'll see how silly you're being."

"Silly?" She stepped aside enough to permit him to squeeze by. The familiar, tangy aroma of his after-shave, the close by warmth of his body, the sadness and futility she saw mirrored in his eyes, all combined to cause her acute pain.

Amy put out her hand, but he sidestepped it. "Okay. You win. If it's silly to care about you, silly to want to be with you, silly to love you with all my heart, then I'm guilty." Her eyes filled with tears, and she blinked them back. She wanted him to stay because he truly cared for her, not because she'd lost control of her emotions.

Mike paused. "Amy, don't. Please."

"Don't what? Don't love you?" She shook her head. "Sorry. It's too late. I already do."

"No." Unyielding, Mike searched her expression as if by sheer strength of will he could undo the magic of the love she claimed belonged to him. "You can't love me."

"Why not, Mike?"

"Because..." He knew his arguments were weak. Still, they were all he had. It had been a long long time since he'd examined them closely, and it suddenly occurred to him that he'd been unraveling their substance ever since he'd met Amy.

What panicked Mike most was his sudden awareness of how vulnerable Amy had made him. To care was to hurt. To pursue personal happiness was to open yourself to emotional destruction. To admit he loved her was to desire the best while waiting with certainty for the worst.

He grasped the knob and opened the door. "Because that kind of thing doesn't work in my life," he said clearly. "It never has."

"It could with me," she said. For a moment, Amy thought she might have reached the acutely sensitive man he kept prisoner beneath his brusque exterior. Then, in one quick movement, he was on his way down the hall. She knew, once the elevator door closed behind him, her chances would be gone. She couldn't let that happen. She had to make him see the truth and admit to the feelings he was fighting so valiantly.

"Wait!" Running down the hall, she abandoned her pride in favor of her future. She wasn't going through life without Mike Dixon!

Mike didn't slow his pace. He was almost to the elevators. Even if Amy did catch up to him, what good would it do if he was so determined to leave that he refused to listen to reason?

There was only one chance left—one tack to take—and Amy took it.

"You're a coward, Mike Dixon!" she yelled after him. "A genuine, class-A coward!" Breathless, she watched him hesitate, then pivot to face her.

The elevator doors slid open behind him and two middle-aged women stood looking into the hall. The shorter one glanced from Mike to the approaching Amy, sensed the electrically charged atmosphere and backed away from the door, visibly relieved as it banged closed and carried her away without Mike.

Amy came to a halt a cautious ten feet from him. "You're afraid to fall in love because you've had some rough experiences. Well, too bad. So have a lot of us."

His knuckles whitened where he gripped the handle of his suitcase. She could barely hear him when he said, "You're thinking of your father?"

"Sure I am." She edged closer. "Do you imagine that I love him less because of what he did?"

She lifted her hands into the air, palms up, in a gesture of desperation. "I *hate* what he did, but the important thing to remember now is that he and Mom both loved me unconditionally. I didn't have to earn their affection. They just gave it." Closer now, Amy refrained from touching Mike.

"Meaning?" His voice rumbled low.

"Meaning you don't have to earn or deserve the love I want to give you. It's free, Mike. No strings attached. No cost."

"Nothing is without cost," Mike reminded her.

Tentatively, she laid her hand on his arm, relieved when he didn't pull away. "You're right. Love does require that you give a part of yourself. But what you're forgetting is that you receive a special part of my heart and soul in return. All you have to do is be willing to take it."

"For me," Mike said quietly, "the taking is the hardest part. It always has been."

"I know." The pleading look in his eyes was so dear it made her insides tie in knots and her heart ache for him. "You could begin by simply giving your love and trust time to take care of the rest."

His voice was a coarse whisper as he fought the last losing battle with his memories. "Oh, Amy. Would you be willing to give me a chance like that?"

As she raised on tiptoe and slipped her arms around his neck she was smiling. "You shouldn't even have to ask."

"And you'll bear with me until I get it right?" Letting his suitcase drop to the floor, Mike placed his hands lightly on her waist. "I'm still not sure I'm capable of loving you the way you deserve to be loved."

"I'm sure," Amy told him. Her hands rested on his chest, her eyes begging for his embrace.

Mike closed his arms around her and buried his face between her neck and shoulder. She smelled like roses. She was right. It was time to quit running from all the good things in life, time he left the past in the past and claimed the blessings of the love clinging so tightly to him at that moment.

It was time to live again. "I'll try," he promised, as a solitary tear fell into the silky softness of Amy's hair. "I swear I'll try."

"You'll make it." Amy gazed into his eyes and found more love than she'd ever dared hope for. "We both will. Together."

Mike kissed her, his lips barely brushing hers in a promise of eternity. "That sounds like you'd accept if I asked you to marry me," he said, holding her away so he could read the honest commitment in her face. This was it—the final test. In spite of her declarations of love, Mike half expected Amy to refuse him.

Tenderly, she stroked his left cheek, then stretched to place a feather-light kiss upon the scar there.

"I've wanted to be your wife for a very long time," she confessed, tracing the scar's ridge with one fingertip. "It's time you had someone you could count on to kiss away all your old hurts."

"There were a lot of them," Mike said.

"I know I have enough kisses," she countered. "I've saved them for you all my life."

Looping his arm around her waist, Mike picked up his suitcase and escorted Amy down the hall. "Then I suggest we get started." He'd begun to grin. "My place or yours?"

"Yours," she said, giggling. "But remember, we have to be at Susan's by two."

"We'll probably be late." Opening the door, he pitched his bag through ahead of them, bent down and swung Amy into his arms.

She clung to his neck as he lifted and carried her across the threshold. "It's not polite to arrive late," she teased.

"No, but it's damned necessary," Mike told her. "I've wanted you for my own since the first day I met you." He kicked the door closed behind them.

"*Now* you tell me."

"If I had told you sooner, it wouldn't have been the same. I had a long way to travel before I could admit . . . I love you."

"We'll go the rest of the way together," Amy vowed.

Smiling as he lowered her gently and set her on her feet, she stepped into his urgent embrace and began to fulfill her promise to kiss away the past.

*   *   *   *   *

A compelling novel of deadly revenge and passion
from bestselling international
romance author Penny Jordan

POWER PLAY

Eleven years had passed but the
terror of that night was something
Pepper Minesse would never
forget. Fueled by revenge against
the four men who had brutally
shattered her past, she set in
motion a deadly plan to destroy
their futures.

Available in February!

Penny
Jordan

At long last, the books you've been waiting for
by one of America's top romance authors!

DIANA PALMER

DUETS

Ten years ago Diana Palmer published her very first
romances. Powerful and dramatic, these gripping tales
of love are everything you have come to expect from
Diana Palmer.

In March, some of these titles will be available again in
DIANA PALMER DUETS—a special three-book collection. Each book will have two wonderful stories plus an
introduction by the author. You won't want to miss them!

Book 1
SWEET ENEMY
LOVE ON TRIAL

Book 2
STORM OVER THE LAKE
TO LOVE AND CHERISH

Book 3
IF WINTER COMES
NOW AND FOREVER

 *Silhouette Books®*

DP-1

READERS' COMMENTS ON SILHOUETTE ROMANCES:

"The best time of my day is when I put my children to bed at naptime and sit down to read a Silhouette Romance. Keep up the good work."

P.M.*, Allegan, MI

"I am very fond of the quality of your Silhouette Romances. They are so real. I have tried to read some of the other romances, but I always come back to Silhouette."

C.S., Mechanicsburg, PA

"I feel that Silhouette Books offer a wider choice and/or variety than any of the other romance books available."

R.R., Aberdeen, WA

"I have enjoyed reading Silhouette Romances for many years now. They are light and refreshing. You can always put yourself in the main characters' place, feeling alive and beautiful."

J.M.K., San Antonio, TX

"My boyfriend always teases me about Silhouette Books. He asks me, how's my love life and naturally I say terrific, but I tell him that there is always room for a little more romance from Silhouette."

F.N., Ontario, Canada

*names available on request

Silhouette Intimate Moments

Available now . . . it's time for

TIMES CHANGE
Nora Roberts

Jacob Hornblower is determined to stop his brother, Caleb, from making the mistake of his life—but his timing's off, and he encounters Sunny Stone instead. Their passion is timeless—but will this mismatched couple learn to share their tomorrows?

Don't miss Silhouette Intimate Moments #317

Get your copy now—while there's still time!

Silhouette Romances®

Diana Palmer brings you an Award of Excellence title... and the first Silhouette Romance DIAMOND JUBILEE book.

ETHAN
by Diana Palmer

In January 1990, Diana Palmer continues her bestselling LONG, TALL TEXANS series with *Ethan*—the story of a rugged rancher who refuses to get roped and tied by Arabella Craig, the one woman he can't resist.

The Award of Excellence is given to one specially selected title per month. Spend January with *Ethan* #694... a special DIAMOND JUBILEE title... only in Silhouette Romance.